Steve Attridge has written a dozen T
TV documentaries, and Feature Films. ᵢₑ ₕₐₛ ₕₐd
scripts produced. Twice a BAFTA nominee, he has also won RTS Awards (Best Drama), Best Film Award (*GUY X*), 2 Writer's Guild Awards (*Billy Webb* and *The Bill*) and TV film awards (*Hawkins*). He won an Eric Gregory Award for Poetry and a slam poetry award. Steve Attridge has 20 books published, including adult fiction, psychological thrillers, children's, history, comedy, and two new books ready to go. His novel, *The Natural Law*, went straight to number one in the Amazon Kindle Singles Bestsellers. Nine of his stage plays have been produced and his theatre show, *Chaos, Carnage and Kulture,* had a successful run at the Shakespeare Birthplace Trust. He has worked as a Writer and Lecturer all over the world, running Masterclasses, short courses and University Courses, including Oxford, Warwick and Sheffield. He ran writing workshops at the New York Public library.

Other titles by Steve Attridge include **The Harrowing of Ben Hartley; Philosophical Investigations; The Natural Law; Beyond Good and Evil** and **The Second Sex.**

"Steve is the best writer of dialogue in the UK." Clive Parsons, Producer.

"Bottom of the List is the funniest, wittiest book I've ever read. It also cleverly explores important issues." Katie Reed, TV Director and Producer.

"Steve is probably the best lecturer on writing in the country." Monica Troughton, Writer, Journalist, Actress.

"One of the leading dramatic talents in the country." Producer and former Head of BBC Series.

"Steve's stage show is the best live theatre I've seen this year." Graham Hardy, Student Arts Promoter.

"Steve Attridge is a rare talent. Prolific, varied, and always worth reading. His comic writing, for example, exceeds Tom Sharpe in breadth and scope, but also brings serious and riveting undertones to the work, so that as you laugh, you are also confronted with insights and telling observations."

Neil Marr, Publisher, editor, journalist.

Behind Closed Doors

Steve Attridge

© Steve Attridge 2013

Steve Attridge has asserted his rights under the Copyright, Design and Patents Act, 1988, to be identified as the author of this work.

First published 2013 by Endeavour Press Ltd.
This edition published in 2016.

For Neil Marr, Father Slade and the ghosts of Anchorhold

Table of Contents

Chapter One	1
Chapter Two	5
Chapter Three	12
Chapter Four	17
Chapter Five	21
Chapter Six	26
Chapter Seven	31
Chapter Eight	36
Chapter Nine	40
Chapter Ten	50
Chapter Eleven	58
Chapter Twelve	63
Chapter Thirteen	66
Chapter Fourteen	70
Chapter Fifteen	73
Chapter Sixteen	78
Chapter Seventeen	84
Chapter Eighteen	88
Chapter Nineteen	92
Chapter Twenty	97
Chapter Twenty One	103
Chapter Twenty Two	107

Chapter Twenty Three	112
Chapter Twenty Four	115
Chapter Twenty Five	120
Chapter Twenty Six	125
Chapter Twenty Seven	131
Chapter Twenty Eight	138
Chapter Twenty Nine	142
Chapter Thirty	151
Chapter Thirty One	154
Chapter Thirty Two	160
Chapter Thirty Three	163

Chapter One

Does God ever wonder why?

The thought passed through the Archbishop's mind as he twirled a large ruby ring on his third finger and looked down broodily at a flock of nuns gliding to chapel like penguins on an escalator. They were all excited he was there. One or two of the younger ones blushed and giggled when the Mother Superior introduced him. Women were, thank God, a complete mystery to him. If only he could say the same of his more...he searched for a word – worldly? Sensuous? Overheated? Filthy minded? – spiritual brothers. Flesh was a river of pain and quivering offal. How could anyone be obsessed with it to the point of slavering cretinism? Here, an unwelcome flashback of Father Dogherty whom he discovered, as a young man, in the seeding shed at the College of the Resurrection, slowly tightening an anvil on his member, holding a picture of Elsie Tanner from Coronation Street in the other hand, and an expression of unholy drooling on his flushed face. The Archbishop shuddered involuntarily. This obsession with women was certainly a mystery, but then God was a mystery too, so perhaps they were connected in some arcane way. No, best not follow that train of thought. There were bigger fish to hook and grill. Rome. Islam. But how? And whom?

The Archbishop was on a whistle-stop tour of Anglican monasteries and Convents, ostensibly to rally and comfort the faithful, crack the whip in certain cases, but he had a far deeper purpose. He had a Vision. It would change the world. But first he needed to take soundings, and to do that he needed a spy. Someone innocuous, someone who barely existed, who could glide in and out of things, a guppy to swim without creating a ripple and report back to his Primate. The Archbishop thought it a mistake to call the head of the Church of England a Primate, as it affiliated him with baboons, monkeys, orangutans and Charles Darwin. Once, on a Feed the World mission in Africa an olive baboon had jumped on the bonnet of his car and stared at him – the small glittery eyes, long platyrrhine nose flattening down to fluted nostrils, the straggly beard – had been disconcertingly like staring in a mirror. That night he dreamed he was knuckle walking across a forest floor, rubbing his anus soothingly on a damp fern, and awoke gasping and hooting, with an alarming and painful erection. He'd recognised some ancient part of himself and only a good dinner, a bottle and a half of claret and several large brandies the next evening at a World Hunger conference in Umlazi township restored a sense of biological and spiritual superiority.

Sometimes it seemed his thoughts were not his own, as if he was a conduit for all manner of strangeness. He had come far, from a North

London Grammar school and an accent bruised with North Circular vowels, to a honey voiced head of the Church who hobnobbed with politicians, media luvvies and God himself. But always, bits of old selves, or perhaps the thoughts of others, entered without knocking.

At tea he gave a blessing and read from Deuteronomy. When he got to 22:5 and intoned the line "The woman shall not wear that which pertaineth unto a man, neither shall a man put on a woman's garment: for all that do so are abomination unto the LORD thy God," there was a distinct giggle from the back of the chapel. The Mother Superior whitened beneath her moustache and looked admonishingly at two young sisters at the back. The Archbishop could swear one of them was wearing false eyelashes and lipstick, but his eyesight wasn't reliable these days. Afterwards he was presented with a calf-bound edition of the Common Book of Prayer by a young sister who smiled sweetly and thanked him for his inspirational visit. She had doe brown eyes and a shy smile, as if embarrassed about occupying the space she was in.

What is your name, my child?

She blushed deeply and said "Sister Annie, most reverend Archbishop."

Annie. Honey. Fanny. Funny. Where were these words coming from? It was the pressure. The pressure of his Vision. He would have to be careful and watch his back. The devil always came from behind.

Then he was gone, whisked away in a brand new silver Mercedes, already dreading his next stop, a small monastic community in Sussex called Rockhold, where he would doubtless eat some tasteless chickpea stew and have to sleep on a coffin-hard bed listening to the monks farting and snoring. There would be no wine, so he asked his driver to stop at an off license on the way. His driver was Father Mack, a former Prison Guard and Episcopalian before his road to Damascus. In the mirror the Archbishop could see Father Mack's eyes dancing like black flames. There was something off key about him, and the Archbishop wondered if his road had been not to Damascus but to Armageddon, but he was so damned useful. He believed in castration and runaway trains. A genius with machines and a fearless spirit who dreamed of a new age of Crusades. Useful but dangerous. There was a place for him in the Archbishop's Vision, but he would have to keep him on a tight leash.

He contemplated his vision, refining it like a sculpture in his mind, a chip here, a brush there, an accentuated curve. It had to be perfect. It would change the world for ever. And he was its architect.

Chapter Two

It was the UK National Anthem that first gave Samir the idea of blowing up St. Paul's and St. Peter's.

When he arrived in England at the age of twelve he couldn't understand why it was called the United Kingdom, when the Scots hated the English, the Welsh hated the English, the Irish hated the English, and the English hated everyone. He listened to the National Anthem to see if it offered some illuminating explanation:

God save our gracious Queen

Long live our noble Queen

God save the Queen

Send her victorious

Happy and glorious

Long to reign over us

God save the Queen

It was complete tosh. For one thing, the queen didn't look gracious or noble, she looked like his mad old neighbour Mrs. Coppins, who drank Guinness, did ballet on the lawn with her knickers around her ankles, and went to bingo with rollers in her hair. Then what on earth did "Send her victorious" mean? Was she going to start a war all on her own? It didn't seem likely. She only had a handbag to fight with, and high heels would be useless in deserts or mountains. The queen's husband was Greek anyway and spent most of his official life insulting foreigners. The Prince of Wales mumbled a lot, talked to plants and at one time expressed a wish to be a tampon.

In a largely godless country where most people were increasingly illiterate, poor and cheated by their government, only the deluded and insane would continue to sing a mournful dirge to a family that had castles and palaces and servants and wealth beyond avarice – no wonder the queen's face was on the currency when she owned so much of it – only the truly simple and mad would think the head of this pampered and piratical family as noble and glorious. No one knew who wrote the anthem so Samir concluded it was probably a German or Spaniard who wanted to mock the English, and had succeeded spectacularly. In any case, there were so many immigrants in England nowadays that the current national anthem was an anachronism. The Polish national anthem would be more appropriate in London hotels. And Jimi Hendrix's 'Voodoo Chile' in Brixton. Samir prided himself on his knowledge of popular culture – it helped to know thine enemy, which is why he was also an avid reader of the Bible. Most Christians knew diddly squat about it. Increasingly Christians couldn't read anyway. The infidels were all illiterate and obese. They had to go.

It was for these, and many other reasons, that he had decided against blowing up Buckingham Palace. In any case, the royal family was usually on holiday or off shooting terrified little birds, or the men drunkenly mounting their polo horses and their mistresses, often confusing the two. It could backfire too. If successful, the English might realise how much better off they were without this superannuated monolith to cart around like some huge, dead animal, and which, zombie-like, still managed to gobble up great chunks of the national budget. The English were indeed a mystery.

So St Peters and St Pauls it had to be. Celebrated symbols of the Christian Church. The nerve centres of Catholicism and Anglicanism, sitting like giant wedding cakes in two of the most distinguished European capitals. This would rock the infidels, and European governments would tie themselves in knots, strangle their peoples with fear – terrorists in every shadow, bombs in every envelope. Fear was the greatest weapon of all, and their own governments would spread it like disease. His enemy was his greatest ally. However, interviewing candidates for the post of suicide bomber was proving more difficult than Samir had imagined.

When Shad (the Happy), his trusted but miserable Number Two, told him there were more applicants than they could ever have hoped for, he thought it would be easy. A day or so interviewing intelligent and passionate young men willing to make the ultimate sacrifice for God and Islam; young men who understood the political and theological necessity for the sacrifice, and would be assured an eternal place in Jannatul Firdaus, the highest level in paradise. Young men who could keep a secret. Young men who would, by their action, help create a global Islamic state, praise God. He had been sorely disappointed. There were a lot of young men who simply wanted to cause explosions, a lot of depressed young men, and a lot of out and out nutters whose brains had been unwired by computer games and European television. Two more to go.

The door opened and Shad, bowing low, ushered in a young man called Wasim. Samir suddenly felt hopeful. The bearded young Wasim entered solemnly, his head bowed, eyes closed, nodding slightly, in the grip of some deep concentration. This was more like it. He was clearly in prayer. This was the sort of steadfast dedication Samir had been hoping for.

"Sit down, my son," said Samir.

Wasim continued to stand, nodding slightly, one foot tapping. Shad prodded him in the ribs and Wasim seemed to come out of a trance. Shad yanked the iPod from around his neck and the little ear pieces popped out like exploding grommets. Wasim looked around, startled to find himself in a small pokey back storeroom of a grocer's shop among herbs, spices, green lentils and international terrorists.

"Sorry. I was, like, list'nin' to Bad Boy Loon e's well wicked and into Islam n'dat, knowwhatImin? Shugga shugga well cool innit?"

Allah give me strength, thought Samir. I wanted a holy warrior and I've been sent a cerebrally challenged Chav.

"My son, why do you want to join our cause?"

Wasim furrowed his brow, his iPod swinging like a necklace of stringy offal.

"Iss for Allah like, innit? We is like well up for it n'dat. Cos like de pagans, de infidels is like dissing us n'dat n' our faith and like my Nan 'ad her benefit cut in 'alf 'cos she like forgot to say my Grandad died two years ago and kept on claiming. Iss like well oppressive innit, praise God."

Samir had a sudden doubt that perhaps he should abandon his Vision, but he closed his eyes, located the little nugget of absolute belief in himself, and was restored. His inner convictions solidified. He looked at Shad, who opened the door and pushed Wasim out. A pulsing drum n'bass soon started, then receded, as Wasim left the shop, stealing a bottle of lucozade on the way.

The last candidate did not inspire confidence. He looked about twelve. Eyes like black olives. Creamy skin. A wisp of beard that would take another three years to grow. Shad stood to one side and indicated the young man.

"Dizhwar. A true believer."

"Dizhwar the strong," said Samir, smiling. "Tell me, my son; are you ready to die for your faith?"

"I shall be glad. I rejoice at the thought of being a martyr in paradise," said Dizhwar.

This was more like it.

"Shad has explained. You go to Rome, and there you change the course of history. You will meet other believers who will give you the explosives and you wait until the cathedral is full. Everything is arranged. Your nerve will not fail? As the moment approaches and you know death is inevitable."

Dizhwar shook his head. He looked a resolute young man.

"And on my next mission, Father Samir, I will sacrifice myself even more for God."

"Your next mission?" Samir searched the young eyes but there was no irony there.

"We will discuss your next suicide mission after…the success of this one. Now wait outside."

Dizhwar bowed and left the room. Shad shrugged when Samir looked at him accusingly.

"He's devout," said Shad.

"He wants to be a serial suicide bomber. Where do you find them, Shad?"

"He's devout," said Shad.

"He's also stupid."

"He's devout."

"Stop saying that. Devout shmout. You can be such an annoying prat sometimes."

He called Dizhwar back in. He told him he would travel to Rome the following Monday, spend the week preparing, then blow St Peters to rubble the following Sunday. Dizhwar asked if he could go on Tuesday instead because on Monday he had to go to the dentist, then help his dad do the big shop for their chippy. Samir told him to get out. Monday it was.

St. Pauls would have to wait. There were over a billion Moslems in the world. Samir wondered if Christians had such problems with their followers.

Chapter Three

Within minutes of arriving the Archbishop knew he'd made a mistake. Rockhold was more a lunatic asylum than a place of peaceful contemplation of the eternal mysteries. As they walked up the Drive, Father Mack puffing furiously on a Park Drive, they suddenly heard sounds of human agony. It sounded as if someone was being whipped to death. Father Mack perked up, his black eyes glittered appreciatively, the possibility of extreme violence, music, meat and drink to his Byzantine tastes. A shed door opened and a monk fell out, stripped to the waist, his back a war zone of bloodied serrations. He staggered to his feet and started lashing himself again with a cruelly thin leather snake whip.

"Oh Sweet Jesus! Welcome to Rockhold..." Crack! "Aaagh! Mercy, Lord!" Crack crack! He kissed the Archbishop's ring. "I am Brother Frank." Crack. "Eeergh! Lord, spare me, your faithful servant." Crack crack. "Thy justice is righteous." Crack. "Father Cray is expecting you, your worship." Crack crack. "No! No! I cry mercy!" Crack crack. "Aggghhhh! We've got salmon sandwiches and a seed cake in your honour." With that Frank the Flagellant staggered bloodily back into the shed and closed the door.

Why does the church attract such nutters? Wondered the Archbishop, looking at Father Mack, who was smirking wheezily to himself, before a coughing fit overtook him and he hawked up a phlegmy yellow gobbet into a goldfish pond and aimed his Park Drive butt at a frog on a lily leaf. God, it was so undignified. I wish I was back in my drawing room in Salisbury eating meringues and doing the Telegraph sudoku, finding safety and occupation in the smooth traffic of numbers in my mind. But there was his vision. He had much to do. This tour. Find his spy. Organise his think-tank symposium of Church Elders. Meet the PM. Do a dreadful TV debate with a fanatical Moslem. All culminating in the Vision. His cross was beginning to seem heavy indeed.

Father Cray was a small, grey, crop-haired man who, whilst remaining a Cowley Father in the High Anglican tradition had flirted with Buddhism, Hinduism, Jainism, Apocalypticism, Taoism, Denominationalism, Messianism, and many more isms that bewildered his brethren in the church. This spiritual eclecticism meant that all manner of strange souls arrived at Rockhold to enjoy the sparsity of Benedictine life. There was Mario, the flying monk, who spent many hours leaping around the garden and flapping his habit like great brown wings; brother Chi the Kung Fu monk who had the alarming habit of starting up from the dinner table and karate chopping the bread board so fiercely it splintered in two; Frank the Flagellant and Brother Gerald, a near blind albino who played the harp so badly the other monks would smile and put in giant ear muffs. Given Gerald's poor sight he never knew. Other less eccentric souls made up the brotherhood of twelve that greeted the Archbishop and Father Mack.

The Archbishop endured being served lardy seedcake and watery tea, listened to Father Cray extol the virtues of herbal elixirs for the bowel, followed by an excruciating ten minutes of discordant plucking from Father Gerald, then he could bear no more. Spending a night there, even with a bottle of claret, was more than he could endure. Inventing an appointment he took his leave and breathed freely as Father Mack swung the Mercedes out of the drive.

"Jeezus, what a bunch of tosspots," muttered Father Mack to himself.

The Archbishop pretended not to hear.

"Only one who looked normal wiz de little feller in de corner."

The Archbishop frowned. What little fellow in the corner? He hadn't noticed anyone. A nonentity.

"Turn the car around," he said.

Ten minutes later they were back in the car, only this time there was a third person. Brother Jocelyn, who had joined the order five years ago instead of going to university, and who wanted nothing more than to merge with God to the extinction of his own personality. Brother Jocelyn, outwardly modest, helpful, self-sacrificing, devout, inwardly full of trumpets and the beating of wings, whom God created as an organ of worship, a vessel of faith. Brother Jocelyn who wanted to spend his life in service, at

Rockhold, or wherever God sent him. It seemed now that his Creator had sent him to this Mercedes with its pot pourri of leather, Mister Muscle upholstery cleaner, cigarettes and something unwholesome from Father Mack. With an embarrassing twinge of pride, Brother Jocelyn felt glad to be singled out like this. It had never happened before.

The Archbishop smiled at Brother Jocelyn on the seat next to him. This was his emissary. His guppy. His spy. Someone nobody noticed. An invisible presence.

Things were looking up. Then like snaked lightning he saw Sister Annie's face. Even better. Two innocents abroad. Who could not love them? Who would not confide the secrets of the heart to them? A shrinking violet monk and an innocent young nun. They would be like Hansel and Gretel. They could be an indispensable source of information on the current Catholic temper. Nuns. Nubs. Nuts. Guns. Snug. Snog. Onus. Anus. He shut his eyes and muttered a short benediction to stifle these unruly words that invaded him.

"Back to St Joseph's," said the Archbishop.

Father Mack muttered something that may have been an obscenity and swung the Mercedes round, cutting in on a Fiesta and almost making it plough into a bus shelter full of people. He chuckled wheezily, his smile like a blood clot. Brother Jocelyn stared out at the clouds high above and thought – the crucified Christ must have looked up at clouds before the sky darkened into a river of blood. A tear trickled down his cheek. I have been chosen. I am unworthy, but God wants me for some mysterious purpose.

"I am sending you to Rome with a young woman, my son," said the Archbishop, and Jocelyn's cheeks flamed. What on earth, or in heaven, could the Archbishop, or God, want him to do with a woman?

Chapter Four

The archbishop was starting to wonder if his choice of guppies was a mistake.

Ever since Sister Annie got in the car brother Jocelyn had regressed to a pale blob of terror. He hadn't looked at her once, and seemed to have trouble with basic human responses, like breathing; whenever she looked at him, his cheeks flamed. They now stood before him in the study at his official residence in Canterbury. Jocelyn had his eyes fixed on the plate of meringues on the Archbishop's desk.

"My children, I am not only primate of all England. In my Ecumenical capacity I look after the Anglican family of other Christian churches in the United Kingdom and abroad. This means over seventy million souls the world over. It is a huge responsibility."

Sister Annie smiled sweetly at him. Brother Jocelyn stared fixedly at the meringues and seemed intent on not breathing. These were not the responses he'd hoped for. He ploughed on.

"In my Inter faith role it is my solemn duty before God to lead Anglican relations with other faiths. It is for this universal purpose that I have chosen you, as the first step in a greater understanding between the great faiths of the world."

Sister Annie smiled sweetly. Jocelyn's eyes crossed.

"I wish you to go to Rome as my emissaries. Listen and learn. Try to understand the world of the Vatican. Tell me what the blessed Catholic brethren and sisters are saying. Be quiet and unobtrusive but alert. Undemanding but attentive. Do you understand? Brother Jocelyn?"

Jocelyn looked up bewildered and felt Sister Annie's eyes on him. He fainted. From a dark corner father Mack emerged, crushed a few daffodils from a vase and threw the water over Jocelyn, who spluttered awake and staggered to a chair. The archbishop put his head in his hands, then looked up at Sister Annie.

"Sister Annie?" He bit into a meringue.

"I understand perfectly, your Grace. You wish us to spy on the Catholics then report back to you."

The Archbishop choked.

"I would have put it less...definitely," he said.

"But it would amount to the same thing, your Grace."

"I wish you to embody the innocence and chastity of your calling."

"Whilst also being sly, dissembling, wily, scheming, underhand, a mask of openness behind which lurks a creature of subterfuge."

"Where do you get all this from?" asked the Archbishop, his beard frosted with meringue crumbs.

"From listening to you, your Grace."

Panic crossed the archbishop's face like a faint electric shock. What was going on here? Where was the shy girl of a few hours ago?

"Sister Fanny, I mean Funny, Annie. Your imagination seems over fertile. Not fertile. I didn't mean to call you...that. I mean, overactive."

"Your Grace, I understand what you mean, and what you want. And that is what I will try to bring you. News, information, gossip, things whispered in shadows – morsels that may help you know how receptive the heart of Catholicism will be to Anglican overtures."

God, this girl was something else. I mutter a few inane words and she gets it instantly. He looked over at Jocelyn, who was recovering. Sister Annie read his thoughts.

"Don't worry. He'll be fine. I'll take him in hand."

And so it was settled. Father Mack took the young pair out to pack for their momentous journey. The Archbishop looked down at an open Bible, wondering how the hell someone like Annie ended up being a nun. She had a disconcerting habit (no pun intended, he thought) of telling the truth, but the truth put so baldly and boldly that it seemed too naked. Human affairs, religious affairs, were often best approached tangentially. God knows the Bible itself was a maze of peculiarities. Leviticus stared up at him, the words a blaze of strangeness: " ...the sheep, the goats, blood and meat, a male without blemish...a female without blemish...And he shall cut it into his pieces, with his head and his fat;...it is a burnt sacrifice, an offering made by fire...turtledoves... young pigeons. And the priest shall bring it unto the altar, and wring off his head, and burn it on the altar...And he shall pluck away his crop with his feathers...It is a burnt sacrifice, an offering made by fire, of a sweet savour to the LORD." He felt both sickened and hungry with all this mention of hacked burnt flesh. He took a bite of a meringue and let its sweetness melt on his tongue. "...if thy oblation be a meat offering baken in the frying pan, it shall be made of fine flour with oil...And he shall lay his hand upon the head of the goat, and kill it...it is a sin offering." He saw himself standing over something dead and dipping his finger in the blood. The events described by the words in Leviticus seemed to stretch across the ages and gather him into themselves. Is this what Christianity really is? The story making you a part of itself. Words were the messengers, but as he was increasingly discovering, words were also the great dissemblers. Meaning was like an unchained lunatic flinging himself against the walls of his cell, refusing to be named, resisting the claims of language.

Now he had his synod with the bishops to decide what to call his vision. Perhaps this would clarify things.

Chapter Five

Father Mack called the diocesan meeting to order by banging so vigorously with a large ecclesiastical gavel that he shattered a glass ashtray. This had the unique effect of ensuring that all the bishops were awake simultaneously.

Sherry had been provided, which was a good thing to create cordiality and ease the tension between forty four Church leaders, many of whom hated and despised each other. However, it was a bad thing for such as Bishop Trunk of Worcestershire, whose secret alcoholism that was public knowledge quickly led to an inflammation of the spirit. He glared at everyone, like a coiled puff adder, waiting for any opportunity to strike.

All looked at the Archbishop. Expectation heated the air. Hostilities, envies, dreads and affections, suspended momentarily. What was this about? He cleared his throat and stood. He looked down at the grainy wood of the oak desk. It was beautiful, patterned like sound waves, like ripples, nipples, like...the word dingle-dangle jumped into his mind, but he swallowed it instantly. Faintly, he had a notion that it had something to do with a scarecrow and genitalia. He must stop this invasion of foul language. Perhaps it was being around Father Mack too much. The man exuded something pestilential. If only he wasn't so damned useful at the more unpleasant duties which ecclesiastical life occasionally necessitated. The Archbishop thought: if only I could reside in a world of beautiful abstractions: vision, faith, salvation, heaven. These were realms uncluttered by the toxic waste of personality. The individual complicated the beauty of abstractions to the point of undermining them completely. He looked around at the strained clutter of faces: Bishop Robin Gumshoe of Essex with his waxy bald pate and enormous wing nut ears with lobes that trembled when he shouted; Bishop Dario Cluster of Rotherham with his halitosis and pickled onion skin; Bishop Bob Strimmer of Lewisham who occasionally took out his false teeth and played with them. Flatulent Bishop Harold "Stinker" Chump of Northumbria. Then the Archbishop was tormented with a wave of love for these poor souls, his flock of shepherds with their own flocks who had flocks of their own, down to the poor wretches who could only look down on their own shadows. People with their jealousies and jockeying for position – he felt a complicated and annoying love for the hopelessness of the individual life. This was why his vision was so imperative for all, for the world, for himself, for the pride in his humility before God. To put abstractions back at the forefront of history, and let all our little lives play out their comedies and tragedies against the universal truths.

"Bishops, friends, I have called this extraordinary synod because it seems to me that we who represent the Church stand at a crossroads. Our Lord himself showed patience when necessary and positive action when imperative. I take as my text for this meeting, this historic meeting, Matthew 28:19: 'Make disciples of all nations, baptizing them in the name of the Father and of the Son and of the Holy Spirit.' The message is clear – go. Don't wait for them to come; don't wait for people to arrive; travel, seek opportunity, hunt converts. God is giving us an imperative global mission, and more specifically the global mission of the crucified and risen Christ. Too long, the church has been passive, self protective, and I say this to you: now, we must go out and transform the world. Utterly, irrevocably."

There was a thud as Arnold Wallop's, The Bishop of Chelmsford, head crashed forward on the table before him. Why on earth did I appoint a narcoleptic bishop? Thought the Archbishop, thinking miserably of the occasion when Arnold had fallen asleep and nearly drowned in a bowl of oxtail soup at the Lord Mayor's dinner, while the Prime Minister made a speech about being alert to the changing modern world. Father Mack cuffed the slumbering bishop's head until he snuffled awake and looked around amazed.

"Have I missed anything?" he asked, licking imaginary soup from his chops.

Only the beginning of a new moral universe, you blundering dildo, thought the Archbishop, then forgave himself for the unkind thought.

He fired a dart of love at the old cretin. He continued, explaining that God had already turned over the soil which they now had to plough and harvest; that good mission needs informed local research, and he was already sending emissaries to test the waters, looking and listening in different contexts; that the end result would be a triangular affinity of faiths in the world – Islam, Catholic and Anglican, with the head of the Anglican Church helping to administer this new world order of co-operating faiths striving together in a spirit of religious reconciliation. Such a triumvirate would be a formidable power and governments would have to think twice before declaring wars, creating hunger and poverty.

He paused. Waited for questions. His beautiful vision had started to find a shape. It had begun. God would provide the tools and the words to fashion it into something tangible. A new world had been conceived. He would be its midwife, father and mother. He would be remembered. His humility. His love. Forever and ever.

"What about the Jews?" asked Bishop Bob Skellion of Yarmouth.

Hornet's nest. Forget 'em, thought the Archbishop. "All in good time, Bishop, all in good time," he said. You'd have thought the unification of Anglicanism, Catholicism and Islam would be enough to be getting on with.

"Are there any questions before we continue?" said the Archbishop.

Forty four brains began their various machinations before him, some ploddingly dull, like slow cooking puddings, others wondering if there would be an opportunity for self advancement or settling old scores, yet others wondering what they weren't being told, and a few genuinely rapt with the thought of a new spiritual empire.

"I tink we're missin' somethin' here," and all eyes were on Father Mack, except Bishop Wallop's, who had fallen asleep again, his head drooling on the lap of Bishop Crumb next to him. Disquietingly Crumb seemed to be enjoying the sensation. An arrow of irritation passed through The Archbishop as Father Mack took to the floor.

Chapter Six

"Fellow Christians," began Father Mack, "Oi'm struck by the im-pli-ca-tions of Matt-chew." He said the name as if it was a sinister web of Machiavellian daggers. "As our Lord Archbishop has said: Matt-chew twenty eight noineteen: 'Make discoiples of all nations, baptoizing 'em in the name of the Father and of the Son and of the Holy Spirit.'" In Matt-chew Ten we are told "Go ye therefore, and teach all nations. Go ye therefore and make discoiples of all nations.""

Here, Father Mack's oil-black eyes took in everyone, including the snoring Father Wallop. What the hell is he up to? Wondered the Archbishop.

"Go – the word imploies an aggressive warfare. The Gospel army mus' move upon the nations. The Lord seeks universal empoire, and sends forth his armies to conquer the world. Ev'ry church and every discoiple must onderstand that they have marchin' orders. Not only is ev'ry Christian commanded to go, but the object is stated. They are to make discoiples of Chroist; not great philosophers or thinkers, but discoiples in Chroist Jesus. We are not just followers but soldiers in Chroist and we must go forth armed to the teeth to take on the infidel! They may have to be conquered before they can be converted, so Oi say we need to blunt our cudgels, sharpen our swords and proime our pistols. " Father Mack said.

Now the penny dropped. Opinion ranged widely. Some looked gleeful at the thought of a scrap with the Pope and Islam, others, including a small group already in the middle stages of senile dementia, had no opinion one way or another. They would be hard put to find the door out of the room, let alone the body strewn gateway to a new heaven on earth. The Archbishop grew florid-faced and stood.

"No no no! Father Mack, we are Christian missionaries, priests in the ways of peace, not religious Rambos, Churchified Che Guevaras with Kalashnikovs out to slaughter others just because they are of a different faith. You will not wilfully misinterpret Scripture at a holy synod just to fulfil some absurd personal fantasy of a bloody crusade."

Father Mack bowed theatrically. "Oi stand corrected, y' worship," he said, and sat down, smirking.

Who did he think he was? He'd settle Father Mack's porridge later.

"I wish Father Mack's remarks to be struck from the minutes. If this should ever get public. My vision is one of peaceful co-operation. Clearly it will need some officiating head, and should this be offered..." he waved a hand munificently, "...but our job today is to agree upon a name for this holy and enterprising venture. It should have dignity, gravitas, fellowship and spiritual purpose. Any ideas?"

A collective scratching of heads and shifting of ecclesiastical bottoms.

"A New Understanding Spirituality," suggested Stinker Chump.

"Anus!" Shouted the now completely ratted Bishop Trunk.

"I beg your pardon?" Asked the horrified Archbishop.

"A New Understanding Spirituality abbreviates to 'anus'," said Trunk gleefully.

"How about 'Church Hierarchies of Peace, Prosperity and Ecclesiastical Rapprochement'?" Suggested the garrulous Bishop Griff Hormone of Cumbria.

"Abbreviation – Chopper!" shouted Trunk.

"How about 'God's Own Beneficent Spirit of Harmonious International Testament of Enlightenment'?" This from Bishop Ted Blank.

"Gobshite!" shouted the gleeful Trunk.

"The International Theistic Spirit," offered Stinker Chump.

"Tits!" Shouted several Bishops.

"What about 'Church Of Combined Knowledge'?" suggested someone.

The Archbishop closed his eyes and put his hands over his ears before Trunk could abbreviate. Where was all this synonymic filth coming from? Had something ancient and dark crept like fog beneath the door and was now busy metamorphosing into verbal sewage? Were all his spiritual brothers in the collective grip of some obscene subtextual devil? He closed the meeting and left Father

Mack sniggering with Bishop Trunk. Rain outside. A chill inside. A prophet in his own country. Reviled. There was a lesson in this. "But I'll be blown if I can see what it is. All I want is a name for my vision." He passed Brother Jocelyn.

"Why not call it Faith?"

The Archbishop stopped. Jocelyn's cheeks flared.

"What did you say?" Hissed the Archbishop suspiciously. Innuendo and mockery were breeding like flies. Nothing was innocent.

"Er, faith, your worship."

"Are you mocking me?"

Jocelyn looked as if he would faint. He shook his head.

"And what might the letters stand for?" asked the Archbishop, sensing there might be a different sort of linguistic trap. "Some profane perversion of the flesh, perhaps? Some human orifice? Some unspeakable violation of the body?"

Jocelyn's eyes widened in horror.

"Er, how about For All In Triumphant Hope?" He said.

The Archbishop stared at Jocelyn, then suddenly beamed. It wasn't a pit of snakes posing as words. It was simple and true. It got to the heart of things. God was guiding him. He had sent this boy. He seemed to see his Vision grow before his eyes, like a jigsaw of nations and peoples moving like mercury, then solidifying into a single shining figure that was something like the Archbishop himself. He put his arm around the confused young monk.

"The pressures of office my boy. We must be vigilant. You caught me off guard. An excellent suggestion. Come to my room for tea and meringues. We'll discuss your Roman Mission."

Chapter Seven

While the Archbishop took the confused young Monk to his drawing room and Father Mack slipped from the synod room to telephone a Sun journalist, Samir looked down at the first line of the Quoran: "This book is not to be doubted." The words seemed to beckon him in. He wondered: Is this what Islam really is? The story gathering you into itself, dissolving the doubts and nightmares of twilight, the harpies of the night. Like the Archbishop he found the world a cheerier place when stripped of the vicissitudes of the individual. He had to fight against the need to be normal, to feel specific sympathies and hatreds, and then dissolve them in the purity of faith, and let that slipperiness of self solidify into conviction. He had to banish himself and become that pure instrument of God. What did it matter that those who would carry out the jihad were weak or stupid; their actions would purify and ensure them a place in heaven. God would be with them so what matter if their heads ached, their bowels trembled? All would be as it should.

He suddenly felt with breathtaking clarity that he had made the right decision to concentrate on St Peters, then St Pauls. America was a wounded eagle, praise God. In time it would become irrelevant, exhausting itself in a dream of control, economically dwarfed by China, consumed with its own story, thinking itself all powerful and never grasping that power is helpless against us. The more power, the more helpless, like a blind giant lumbering around the world. They could not even learn from their own story of David and Goliath. There was no need to worry about America. That is my cleverness, he thought. That is why I shall destroy Rome first. The ancient European cultures. The beginnings of Christianity. Once cultured but now drowning in a swamp of reality TV, obesity and bubblewrap thought.

The next day he smiled at the Sun headline: 'Bishops to Batter Unbelievers.' The brief article went on to state that at a Church synod called by the Archbishop of Canterbury it had been agreed that there should be a global mission to convert Moslems to Christianity at all costs. Things were warming up. What better justification for the destruction of St Peters? Shad the Happy called in Dizhwar for a final briefing; he looked even younger than before.

"You have prepared yourself for your mission, my son?" asked Samir.

"Yes, Imam. I've bought a new toothbrush, my Mum's bought me loads of pants – I told her it was a holiday – and I've sold my Wii to my cousin Ahmed."

Samir looked at Shad, who shrugged.

"Dizhwar. Samir means prepared yourself spiritually and in your mind for the great sacrifice," he said.

"Right. Yes, Imam, I am ready to die for Allah as often as he wants me to."

A slight tic started below Samir's left eye.

"To return having failed would bring shame to you, your family, and to me for all eternity," he said.

"I won't fail. I am honoured to be chosen, Imam, and I will serve God in any way that he wishes. I will cut out my own eyes, tear off my ears, pull out my own tongue and liver and spleen and kidneys and all other bits, hack off my own hands and tear out my heart..."

"Yes yes, very good. But just stick to the mission in hand," interrupted Samir.

Shad looked puzzled.

"How would you tear out your heart if you'd just hacked off your hands? And how would you hack off the second hand anyway? Unless you tied a knife to your foot and ..." he said, but Samir interrupted.

"Shad! Silence," he said, wondering why people always strayed from the point. Why couldn't they just shut up and do what he said? Why couldn't people behave in straight lines, instead of confusing things with their own ludicrous personalities?

"Do you have any questions before you leave for the city of the Catholics?" He asked.

"Yes, Imam, I am very frightened of aeroplanes. I think I will hide in the toilet. If I die of fright in there is it a bad thing if one dies whilst on the toilet? Is it Haram to die on the toilet?"

Samir looked at the boy for signs of sarcasm. There were none in those dark limpid pools.

"I am not aware of any divine text informing us that dying on the toilet indicates whether a person is good or bad. Moreover some classical scholars in Islam have died whilst urinating or excreting. Death is in the Hands of Allah. It makes no difference because Allah promises to account us according to our actions, not where or when ones dies. Is there anything else?"

"Yes, Imam, my cousin Saddam is always picking his nose and I find it disgusting. Sometimes he even eats it. How should a good Moslem clean his nose, Imam?"

This boy was decidedly weird. He was about to die in the act of delivering a mortal and immortal blow to the infidel, and all he could think about was toilets and nose picking.

"To pick and clean your nose is permissible as long as it is in private and only with your left hand. You must then wash before shaking the hands of others. So picking your nose to clean it is permissible and even recommended in wudu and ghusl. However, to eat this would be to eat Najasah, or impurity, which is Haram."

"What about the washing of private parts in public, Imam?" asked Dizhwar.

"Enough with the questions. You have to get to the airport. Bless you, my son."

He kissed him on the forehead and told him to say his prayers regularly until the great day in Rome, then dismissed him. The telephone rang. It was the Archbishop of Canterbury. He sounded very stressed and asked if Samir had seen today's headlines. It was all a terrible mistake. The BBC had offered a high profile slot for him to meet with a Moslem spokesperson to clear the air and show that Church officials from both faiths were in accord, that friendship, respect and agreement was the currency between Islam and Christianity. Would Samir like to be the representative for Islam? Samir smiled. It was too perfect.

"Of course your reverence and we will show the world how much we have in common. It will be an occasion of friendship and clarification. How the great faiths of the world can live in harmony and co-operation."

He could hear the Archbishop sigh with relief. Feel him relax. Now he really had him by the short and curlies.

Chapter Eight

Arty Grimnob was feeling very pleased with himself. It wasn't the two salaries that the BBC was currently paying him; one for being Head of Creative Channeling, one for being Artistic Director of the Aesthetic and Documentary Thinktank, nor the illegal pension he'd awarded himself when he stopped being Chief of Drama Initiatives and Inventive Directives. It wasn't the OBE he'd exhaustively lobbied and bullied for. It wasn't the numerous internal awards he'd been given by the BBC when he was Controller of BBC Internal Awards. No, it was that he sniffed a BAFTA. Those bastards had refused him one so far, despite the numerous lunches, magnums of Dom Perignon and Kristal he'd dispensed far and wide, paid for by the beeb, of course. He'd persuaded, charmed, occasionally bedded, promised commissions, even tried a few terrifying homosexual advances, but the imbeciles had ignored him.

All that was about to change. As Director of Significant Current Events, for which he received another salary, he had chosen himself over considerable opposition to host the discussion between the Archbishop of Canterbury and Samir Abaza, Spokesperson for the Islamic population of Great Britain, with a contextual documentary to follow. He had seriously considered all other applications for the job, but finally concluded that he was by far the most intelligent, informed and charismatically appropriate man for the job, and if anyone disagreed they could shove it up their arses. This programme had BAFTA all over it.

He leaned back in his enormous swivel chair that always threatened to engulf him, put his chubby little legs on the desk, and puffed on a thin cigar. His mind wheeled as he created the programme in his mind. He held up his baby-fat fingers to frame an imaginary shot of himself poring over the Quoran, brow creased deeply to create the illusion of thought. Another of him gazing up at St Pauls and pondering the great Christian mysteries. And now here he is staring moodily at the Kaaba in Mecca. Yet another of him cradling a glass of Louis Jadot Pouilly-Fuisse and writing something of enormous profundity and significance in an ancient, leather bound book. If only he had some hair left. Perhaps he should grow a beard? No, David Bellamy had a beard and was now in the Siberia of broadcasting. And look at Rolf Harris. This documentary section would come in the second part of the programme and would run for approximately two hours. The first part would be a fifteen minute exchange between the two holy men with Arty controlling it all. Of course, the camera would be mostly on him as he nodded sagely or smiled ruefully (indicating polite disagreement) while those two blathered on.

There was one small problem. Two actually. He knew fuck all about Islam and very little about Christianity. Christ knows he knew little enough about his own Jewish faith. However, this could be an advantage in television. People were no longer interested in knowledge, only in opinion, so all he needed was a minion to Google a few sexy soundbite remarks which he would then read from an idiot board when the two old religious carthorses had wittered on for too long. God, life was good. It was such a blessing to be gifted, creative and clever in so many diverse fields. Sometimes he amazed himself.

Arty buzzed in Jems, a sassy and ambitious little number with tits like inflated bell tents. He had been promising her for a year that she could go on a Producer's training course, in the hope that she would see that she needed to put out, preferably over his desk, in order for it to happen. Either she was thick or, for some peculiar reason, she didn't find Arty attractive. She was wearing a t-shirt that was fighting a losing battle to contain her magnificences. Arty couldn't keep his eyes off them. He explained that he needed a few choice remarks about Christianity in the Modern World and about Islam – central tenets of belief, including a few in Arabic too, to show how cultivated he was and impress the hell out of the viewers. He came round the desk and put a hand on her shoulder as he talked. She seemed to flinch. The chubby fingers caressed an ear and he told her how attractive she was. He could feel her withdraw. What the hell was the matter with the girl? Perhaps she was a lesbian. Or just frigid. He dismissed her. She turned at the door.

"Oh, Arty. About that Producer's course?"

He looked at her blankly.

"I'm not fucking Father Christmas. You'll go on a course when you've shown me your...potential. Which looks as if it might be never. In the meantime just get on with your job."

For a moment she looked as if she would cry, but the steel set in her and she left, closing the door with deliberate care. Little bitch. Women were so unreasonable. They seemed to expect the world to fall in their laps without having to earn it. Incredible. He leaned back and imagined the camera zooming in on his visionary eyes as he gazed at a religious icon.

Chapter Nine

Brother Jocelyn's mouth felt dry. His palms were sweaty. His forehead throbbed. His ears hummed. He had brought along a book called *The New Science* in the hope that it would be very boring and numb his mind to the closeness of Annie, but the words blurred on the page. He looked out of the Boeing 707 window and envied the clouds. If only he was out there, in the cool rush of air, and not sitting next to Sister Annie. There were moments when their garments actually touched and he thought he might pass out. One of the great blessings of entering Rockhold was the absence of women. At the age of thirteen he had found the onslaught of adolescence a terrifying experience. Waking up one night with a thundering erection that left a permanent kink in his spiderman pyjamas, was bad enough, but going into his parents' bedroom to show them his aberration had proved a mistake. They were in the middle of a complicated sexual maneuver involving the use of seven pillows, a vibrating purple loofah and a great deal of body lotion and huffing and puffing.

Thereafter the world seemed a sexual minefield. Anything erect made him think of the death of his superhero and his own lost childhood; anything soft and yielding, from fish pie to wet cement to rice pudding, sent his pulses racing and his thoughts into a turmoil of naked, writhing women. Even the moon looked like a giant breast lamenting the loss of a nipple. He dreaded the sight of raw meat and figs. He prayed that this terrible affliction might be taken from him and promised in return a life of abstemious devotion and, in his infinite wisdom, God granted this wish. The next morning everything had returned to normal. The world was full of soft and hard surfaces, but that's all they were, and contained no sinister associations. He joined the Church choir, sang his voice-cracking praises to the everlasting, and gave himself up entirely to God. He endured the misery of school, then went to Rockhold where God held him safe from all that scattered his brain, and where girls were shadows on the streets, there but always at a distance. It was sublime. He was happy. Something in him had disappeared and he was glad. After all, wasn't that central to faith – that you sublimated the flesh to things of the spirit, that you let God eclipse your own carnality and cleanse your mind of filthy thoughts? "The desires of the flesh are against the Spirit, and the desires of the Spirit are against the flesh" St. Paul said. It was a simple choice and Jocelyn had made his.

The more he prayed and meditated the more he realised Paul included just about everything as a carnal sin: fornication, impurity, licentiousness, drunkenness, carousing, idolatry, sorcery, enmity, strife, jealousy, anger, selfishness, dissension, party spirit, envy, the lust of the eyes, pride of flesh. In fact he went further: "...if by the Spirit you put to death the deeds of the body you will live." So in fact anything physical – eating, looking, hearing, brushing your teeth, walking, sleeping, even things like listening to music, or reading because you used your eyes, had the stink of sin on it. According to this way of understanding life, everything takes on the character of carnal sins and of the sensual enjoyment connected with the flesh. Jocelyn took up this crusade against the physical universe with utter dedication. He sought nothing less than the annihilation of the physical. Arguably, this meant the best thing he could do, the only logical thing he could do, would be to kill himself, but that in itself was a physical act and therefore a sin. So he kept it all at a distance and determined to live in a spiritual bubble where something like peace resided.

Now he was seated next to a woman. A nun, but underneath her habit, a woman. Worse, he needed to go to the toilet, itself probably a carnal sin, and to do so he would have to get past Sister Annie, which meant a universe of intimacy that could set him back years. Spiderman would do it by walking across the ceiling, but Spiderman was dead. He squirmed miserably, and reminded himself that the Archbishop himself had chosen him for this fact finding mission in service of the church. God's own emissary on earth had singled him, little Jocelyn, out and perhaps all this physical torment was a necessary part of it, a trial of the flesh. He thought that if he meditated on the Cross he might endure this flight. Perhaps the need to go to the toilet might even vanish. He closed his eyes and imagined the Cross bathed in blood red light, the laughter of the centurions, the weeping of the Holy Mother, the agonies of our Lord and the thieves. The gash in the side. The sponge. Vinegar. A figure standing beside Mary, looking up at his Agony. Despite the distance he could feel her warmth, her sweet breath. His misty eyes cleared and he saw it was her. Annie. Sister Annie, there at the final hour.

"If you want to go to the bathroom, Brother, why don't you? I'm not so fat as you can't slip by."

She was so close. Her eyes like Bourneville chocolate. In great confusion and no little physical distress, he edged past her, the rustle of cloth, the flesh beneath, everything unravelling. The engaged sign lit at the toilet. He waited outside miserably, feeling the eyes of everyone on him, Brother Jocelyn, desperate to pee. The air hostess noticed his discomfort and smiled. Jocelyn blushed plum purple. He leaned his face against the door and hoped the plane would crash, then uttered a quick prayer asking to be forgiven for such a thought. He could hear someone inside. What on earth were they doing? He listened closely. It was a constant babble from someone who was clearly in some sort of distress. He turned to the hostess.

"Excuse me, I think there might be some sort of problem in here," he said.

The young woman, standing dangerously close to him, listened at the door.

"Someone's talking very quickly. There must be more than one in there, unless they're using a phone illegally," she said.

She knocked on the door. The voice stopped.

"Hello? Is everything alright in there?" She asked.

A pause. She rapped on the door.

"Hello? Could you open this door please?"

The babbling started up again, only louder and more furiously. The hostess used the intercom to summon a male colleague. He rapped on the door but the babbling therein continued. He went into the pilot's cockpit and Jocelyn heard them talking. His need to pee was becoming desperate. The young man returned and knocked on the door again. No response.

"Stand back, please," he said to Jocelyn.

He barged the door, which bowed but held. A few passengers looked up, alarmed. A smell of danger leaked down the gangway. The hostess tried to block what was happening and reassure those passengers nearest that everything was OK. The young man took a run at the door and flung his weight at it. The door fell in. Jocelyn got a glimpse of a young man kneeling with his head down the toilet bowl. The door crashed on his back with the steward on top of it. Jocelyn stood watching, horrified. The steward scrambled up and dragged the door from the prostrate, struggling Dizhwar. He had been kneeling before the toilet bowl praying fervently that God would not allow the plane to crash, when the combined weight of the door and the steward lurched him forward and rammed his head down the toilet bowl, where it was now stuck fast, his skinny legs thrashing out behind him. His arms embraced the toilet bowl, as if he was being devoured head first by a metal mouthed monster. Every time he tried to breathe in he got a nose and mouthful of acrid water. He was drowning.

It took a moment for the Steward to take in what had happened. Then he grabbed Dizhwar's legs and tried to pull him out, but his head was jammed down to the gills. There was a great deal of spluttering and gurgling and kicking. Dizhwar was becoming frantic. The Steward turned to Jocelyn.

"Grab a leg. Help me yank him out."

Jocelyn grabbed a leg which promptly kicked him in the balls. His desire to pee doubled as the pain seared up his spine. The steward grabbed the other leg while the stewardess got a bar of soap and rubbed it around the toilet bowl where Dizhwar's head was stuck fast. Hopefully this would create added slippage.

"OK. We're going to count to three then pull!" Shouted the Steward to Dizhwar.

"Glurp splub ucky ucky phlerm!" replied the young man.

"Is that Arabic or something?" Asked the Steward.

"I think it's the noise someone makes when they're nearly dead," said Jocelyn.

The Steward counted one, two, three, then they both yanked and heaved. Dizhwar would not budge, and his arms started flailing wildly. He accidentally pressed the flush button and the toilet flushed over his head. The gurglings and splutterings became more panicky. A large florid faced man appeared eating a chicken and bacon sandwich.

"Ron. I'm a plumber," he said.

"We've got an emergency here, Ron. What do you suggest?"

Ignoring Dizhwar's gargling and bubbling, he leaned down to look at the toilet. He shook his head sadly. "I dunno what muppet decided to install these but they're a bugger to shift. See, if you'd used traditional porcelain or vitreous china, say your American Standard 3708.216.020 H2Option Siphonic Dual Flush Round Front, or the pricier but, in my view, ultimately more durable, elongated Toto, twelve-inch rough-in, elegant low profile design, power gravity system, large water surface, and 1.6 GPF, then we'd be laughing."

"Why? Asked the stewardess.

"Cos we could take a monkey wrench to the fucker and smash it in, but what you got 'ere in these chrome plated, look...see this? What you got 'ere is a chrome 'exagon 'alf inch nipple which some comedian, don't ask me why, 'as attached to an isolator valve."

"And what does that mean?" She asked.

"If I tell you that I once did a woman down in Tunbridge Wells. Tell a lie, Canterbury East. Nice woman. Her poodle got its arse rammed down the chrome plated. Don't ask me why. Ours not to reason, though I surmised it'd been trying to emulate its mistress, as it were. Nervy breed poodles. It's the French in 'em, see? Very volatile. Anyway, long story short. She 'ad an 'exagon 'alf inch nipple too and it took me all morning armed to the teeth with a set of open ended ratchet rings to ease it off the double webbed flange and pull the bastard off."

"Was the poodle OK?" asked the steward.

"Traumatised rectum and permanent kink in its short and curly, but it could have been worse."

Jocelyn saw with horror that the legs had stopped kicking and had progressed to involuntary twitching.

"I think we ought to do something," he said.

"Interesting fact about your porcelain bowls, though. They're prone to heavy sweating," said Ron.

"Toilet bowls don't sweat!" said the Steward.

Ron smiled knowingly.

"You're not the first to question it. See, toilet bowls sweat due to the fact that the air round the toilet is considerably warmer than the temperature of the toilet water. This creates condensation and causes the toilet to sweat. And you know what that can lead to, don't you?"

"What?" Asked the Stewardess.

"Mould and mildew. I could tell you stories about what I've seen growing in some toilet bowls would make your hair curl. 'Ad a woman out Epping way once. Tell a lie, Walthamstow it was. What I found when I got my rubbers down her bowl and round 'er u bend'd make a camel puke."

"I don't want to hear this," said the Stewardess.

Ron chuckled. "S'alright. Long story short. I 'ad the solution in me lunch bucket."

They all looked at him.

"Coca cola. See, the old citric acid is death to organic stains on vitreous china. Tricks of the trade."

Dizhwar's legs were now limp.

"I think he might be dead," said Jocelyn.

Ron tapped the chrome toilet bowl knowingly.

"See, if you 'ad a back flush installed, that would torpedo 'is 'ead out from down under, as it were, but as it is..."

"What?" Asked the steward.

"You're basically buggered," said Ron, taking a bite of his sandwich and giving a last professional shake of the head at the inept plumbing arrangements. He looked at the Stewardess. "When you got a minute, love, a lager for me and a white wine for the wife. J56 and 57 on the right there." He sauntered off back to his seat.

The three of them looked at Dizhwar's legs. The Steward could see his pay rise going the same way as Dizhwar. The Stewardess looked at Jocelyn's brown habit.

"Can't you pray or something?" She asked.

Jocelyn closed his eyes. Dear Lord, have mercy on us sinners and help us free this poor soul from his predicament. He opened his eyes. He and the Steward each grabbed a leg while the Stewardess straddled Dizhwar and held his shoulders. One, two, three, then they all gave a last mighty heave. Muscles bunched and stretched, a collective groan, a breaking point loomed, then miracle of miracles as Dizhwar's head came free with a flatulent plop so loud people jumped from their seats at the back of the plane. Jocelyn careered back into the drinks trolley, the Steward on top of him, and on top of them the Stewardess still riding Dizhwar's back like a raunchy cowgirl on a truculent stallion. This tangle slowly unraveled and they stood looking at Dizhwar on the floor, wet, in shock and hyperventilating. Acting on instinct rather than medical knowledge, the Stewardess slapped him round the face and the Steward threw a cup of water over his face. His startled eyes open, now bloodshot and swollen. He was back. Almost. Jocelyn raced into the toilet and achieved a personal first, a public pee.

Half an hour later Dizhwar was festooned between Annie and Jocelyn. He had barely spoken, except to refuse a brandy. Something had altered in his frontal lobes. Whenever he closed his eyes he was back there, trapped, unable to breathe, his eyes full of watery blackness, the world a faraway tinny echo of voices and the amplified roar of engines. This was hell. He had looked into it and he knew – he must never sleep again or it would claim him for good. God had shown him this and he must obey.

Chapter Ten

The studio shone like a freshly boiled egg. Arty had spent the whole of the previous day choosing an outfit, having a banana and lemon juice facial exfoliation, his eyebrows dyed a fierce black, an effleurage back and neck massage and a magnificent hand job from Kim, an IT Assistant in the Department of Televisual Innovation, newly created by Arty himself and of which he was Acting Head, with yet another salary. He had spared no expense of taxpayer's money in preparing himself for this great moment. Three chairs, the one in the middle on a subtle podium to give him that extra height, and a photographic backdrop – a huge blow up of Arty himself looking serious and concerned. The Director had complained that it would detract from the discussion and might be viewed as a personal ego trip. The solution was simple. Arty sacked the Director and decided to direct it himself. He was already producing it, as well as being the star, so it made sense, especially as he knew how the programme should look and sound, with a clarity apparently denied to others. It had worked brilliantly before, in his ground breaking documentary on Michelangelo in which the artist was mentioned twice and Arty three hundred and fifty times, mostly by Arty himself, and in his epoch defining interview with dramatist Donald Pooter, in which Arty's questions, which he sometimes answered himself, took up nine tenths of the programme. He told the Assistant Director to keep the camera on him when he was speaking, and also when he wasn't, to get his reaction shots. The AD asked if there were to be no shots of the Archbishop and the Muslim Priest. Arty relented and said fleeting shots were permissible but no more than five seconds max, then back to Arty.

Ten minutes before the programme the three luminaries are seated. Arty in the centre, having a last dust and powder from make-up, the Archbishop nervous but pleased; this will smooth over the nightmarish newspaper reports. He had confronted Father Mack, who denied contacting the press, so he would have to go through the wearisome task of vetting all his bishops to discover the identity of the whistleblower. Samir smiles over at the Archbishop. His colours are flying. It is the lull. Three men each with a different script for the next hour. And now the moment arrives. It is countdown and Arty looks at number one camera with an expression he has spent years cultivating. A hint of a smile but the eyes oozing sincerity and soul, as if he has just saved a busload of children from death on a mountain road. In fact, this is the very image he likes to dwell on when in front of a camera, which is often. How he actually saved the children is a bit hazy, but it is the expression on his face that counts. The AD thinks it makes him look like a constipated toad.

And now they are away. Arty reading the idiot cards, his shortsighted eyes slightly screwed up, but knowing this gives an air of gravitas to his demeanour. He gets up steam. The kneejerk reactions of the popular press. This programme putting the record straight. A moment of historical magnitude. Two of the greatest spiritual institutions on earth. Reconciliation. Mutual respect. Sharing of values. Both religions have the same ancient prophets, including Jesus Christ.

The Archbishop wonders if Arty is ever going to shut up. Finally he does. He turns to him.

ARTY: Archbishop. This report in the popular press?

ARCHBISHOP: A foolish misunderstanding. I called a synod of bishops and we discussed ways of building bridges with the great Moslem faith in England.

ARTY: So no talk of war, persecution?

ARCHNISHOP: (Laughing) Absolutely not. All nonsense. We are ambassadors for peace, which is the message of Jesus Christ.

SAMIR: (Joins in the laughter)

ARTY: Imam Samir, you accept that this supposed talk of war is just a bit of scaremongering to sell a few more copies of The Sun?

SAMIR: I think it's an irrelevancy. What was Rupert Murdoch's office catchphrase? "Keep 'em angry – keep 'em stupid!" What interests me more is that it would be odd if the venerable Archbishop and his happy band of thugs were not busy planning violence against the Moslem population.

(Smile fades on the Archbishop's face as this sinks in)

ARTY: I'm sorry?

SAMIR: Christianity is a litany of war mongering. Jesus says "I come not to bring peace, but to bring a sword," and "I have come to cast fire upon the earth; and how I wish it were already kindled!" It seems to me if the Archbishop were to read his own scriptures and take them seriously he would be plotting a holocaust.

(A ripple of panic in the studio)

ARCHBISHOP: You are taking those remarks out of context. Jesus Christ is the prince of peace.

SAMIR: "Do you suppose that I came to grant peace on earth? I tell you, no, but rather division." In or out of context these are inflammatory remarks. Literally so.

(Arty looks serious and troubled at camera)

ARCHBISHOP: (Looks as if he might cry) The mission of Christianity is one of forgiveness and love of humanity. Our God is a just God.

SAMIR: I go back further. The Old Testament. Samuel Chapter 15: "Go now and put Amalek to the sword, putting to the curse all they have, without mercy: put to death every man and woman, every child and baby at the breast, every ox and sheep, camel and ass." Even the poor bloody animals get it in the neck in your religion of love and forgiveness. And The Lord is my shepherd. What does the shepherd do? Fattens the sheep and then sells them to be slaughtered and eaten. This is what your faith amounts to? Skinned, hacked to bits, cooked and eaten because you are stupid enough to trust the shepherd?

(The Archbishop, shocked to the root, fights back a desire to make tit for tat comments about Islam)

ARCHBISHOP: You are distorting everything!

SAMIR: Hosea, Chapter thirteen: "Samaria will be made waste...they will be cut down by the sword, their little children will be broken on the rocks, their women who are with child will be cut open." This is not a benign God, it is Freddie Kruger. No wonder you ate our babies during your cursed crusades.

ARTY: (Reading from the idiot cards) Two great faiths, two church leaders, who find they can speak with one voice. Perhaps the lesson here...

ARCHBISHOP: (Interrupting) Why, in God's name, do the crusades have to be dragged in? Here we are, in the twenty first century, still blaming each other for the foolish and violent mistakes of our ancestors.

SAMIR: Your ancestors. All time is present to us.

ARTY: (Still reading) Two men who share one vision...

ARCHBISHOP: I will not stoop to remind you that atrocities were committed on both sides.

SAMIR: You just stooped. Your absurd faith is based on cannibalism, vampirism and murder. Eat, this is my body, drink, this is my blood, you crucified me, now consume me. You should dress like Count Dracula.

ARTY: (Still reading) I myself can see how the two belief systems cohere...my own understanding is that...

ARCHBISHOP: Not cannibalism, communion! Remembering the Last Supper. Not murder – sacrifice. Redemption.

SAMIR: Look at your culture. Soap operas, obesity, women who dress as prostitutes, alcohol and drugs. This is redemption? This is Gomorrah.

ARTY: If I can offer a few thoughts of my own in Arabic. (Reads carefully) Knt Jml Kbyr al-Ānf Mʻ al-Ḥmār ad-D•hwn.

(SAMIR suddenly stops and looks at ARTY, who smiles at him)

SAMIR: What did you say?

ARTY: (Reluctantly puts on his specs to read again) Knt Jml Kbyr al-Ānf Mʻ al-Ḥmār ad-D•hwn.

SAMIR: Now I understand. This programme is simply an opportunity to insult the Moslem population. You and this Dracula priest have set it up between you.

ARTY: I don't understand.

SAMIR: You can speak Arabic?

ARTY: (Defensively) Yes. A little.

SAMIR: Then you know what you just said.

ARTY: Yes. Er. (Looks through notes) Understanding is the first step to heaven.

SAMIR: Ha! What you just said was: You are a big nosed camel with a fat arse.

ARCHBISHOP: Oh my God.

ARTY: (Squinting at a new idiot card) Ah. This is what I really meant. (Reads) Ldyk Wjh Mthl Bwm Qrd al-Bābwn Wāldmāgh Mn Khyār.

ARTY smiles at camera, then at SAMIR.

ARTY: We are all one in the light of God.

SAMIR shakes his head.

SAMIR: No. You have a face like a baboon's bum and the brain of a cucumber.

ARCHBISHOP: Oh my God.

ARTY: But I don't understand.

SAMIR: I do. This was planned. You have insulted me and every Moslem in the world.

Samir strides from the studio. A door slams. The Archbishop looks at Arty as if he would like to skin him alive and feed his entrails to cockroaches. Arty stares meaningfully at the camera wondering why the hell the idiot cards have stopped appearing. He will sack so many people. The BBC will be a killing field before he is done. The cameras should have been cut long ago. The programme should have been blacked out at the first sign of trouble. Why did this not happen? Simple. Arty had made too many enemies. The AD had winked at the camera operator, who winked at the sound man. The Producer told his PA to black out the programme. She told an engineer, who told his assistant, who happened to be the Director sacked by Arty, and who ignored the instruction. And so it was that Arty Grimnob attained the universal notoriety he so craved. Jems,

Arty's thwarted assistant, who wrote the Arabic idiot cards, was already on a bus home, thinking that there were better places than the BBC to work. It had been worth it. Arty's epitaph would surely read: "In loving memory of the dumpy little dickwit who did his ignorant best to cause global mayhem."

Chapter Eleven

Jocelyn and Annie were met at a steamingly hot Ciampino by Father Giuseppe, a jocular little man who liked ice cream and his own jokes. He ushered them to a waiting Mercedes. The interior was deliciously air conditioned. Father Giuseppe sat next to the driver and looked back at them.

"Benvenuti, my children. Such a pleasure. Ah, I have the many fond memories of England. Rain, curry, everyone on benefit except for the Polish immigrati who run the hospitals. Ha ha!" He squeezed Annie's hand a little too long. She looked unperturbed. Jocelyn wanted to offer Dizhwar a lift but as soon as they were through passport control two men wearing ray bans, dark jackets, sandals and traditional white Moslem cloths met him and spoke in whispers. Dizhwar was still stupefied by the toilet incident but the two men who whisked him away didn't look as if they would be taking him to a trauma counsellor. Jocelyn wondered if they were relatives or friends, perhaps associates. During the flight, he found refuge in speculative observation; following the toilet disaster, he spent most of the flight scrutinising the profiles and backs of heads of other passengers, wondering what the purposes of their journeys were, what the contours of their hopes and fears and dreams. Initially he did this to distract his thoughts from circling around Annie like a moth, and from the nearness of her body, but then he quite liked the activity for itself. He squinted so hard at times that Annie wondered if he was shortsighted, or slightly mentally deficient.

He stared long and hard at the balding dome of a man three rows in front and decided that he was a sales executive going to Rome in the hope of closing an important deal – something to do with fruit and jams. He thought the man was separated from his wife and worried constantly that his children might stop loving him, or worse, come to prefer the new man in their mother's life. He felt sorry for him and wished he could offer some comfort, but approaching him and saying that he'd learned all this from contemplating his bald patch might be seen as bad manners. Jocelyn realised he didn't really know how to act in the world. Rockhold had been easier. There were rules. The days unfolded seamlessly in a ritual of prayer and indulging the lunacies of the monks. This was all infinitely more confusing. He wondered if it was sinful in some way to take such a speculative, voyeuristic interest in others like this, but then, as he discovered in the Letters of Paul, you only had to open your eyes in the morning to commit all seven carnal sins. He closed his eyes and asked for forgiveness for such a flippant thought. Being in the world was to be snared in barbed wire.

"Penny for your thoughts, brother," said Sister Annie, smiling sweetly.

"I was thinking about the deadly sins," said Jocelyn.

"All seven. You must have a very fertile imagination," she said guilelessly.

Jocelyn blushed to his roots and felt giddy. He stared at the back of the driver's head and thought of goats and chickens and a dead body, the blood from a terrible wound staining the straw beneath him. What did it mean? Then he saw a man running away from the barn. The name Alberto dropped like a stone in Jocelyn's mind.

They drove along the Via Tunica around the high walls of the Vatican city, then the Via Paulo V1 and into St. Peter's Square. The car parked and they got out into the heat. Jocelyn looked at the basilica, the heart of Christianity. It was immense. A centre of the world and a portal to the everlasting.

"It looks like a giant wedding cake," said Sister Annie cheerfully.

Jocelyn found her puzzling, almost irreverent, yet her face sparkled radiance, and she had taken holy orders: how could anything but purity and faith dwell behind those beautiful eyes? Was it a sin to call them beautiful? Probably, especially if you were St. Paul, although surely there was a place for appreciating the lovely without falling headlong into a pit of carnality? He realised he was looking intently at her and turned away. Two striped and shining Swiss Guards approached, their silk pantaloons billowing like carnival sails. Father Giuseppe explained that the Guards had served the papay since the sixteenth century and pointed to the Last Stand battlefield where in 1527 a hundred and forty seven of the hundred and eighty nine Guards, including their commander, died fighting the forces of Holy Roman Emperor Charles V during the Sack of Rome in order to allow Clement VII to escape through the Passetto di Borgo; Jocelyn noticed that the good father kept his eyes firmly on Sister Annie and seemed to be speaking only to her. The Guards stood by patiently.

The sad driver looked down and said nothing. Jocelyn suddenly knew.

"He was your father. I'm so sorry," said Jocelyn.

The driver looked at him quizzically. Father Giuseppe translated in Italian to the driver, whose mouth opened in astonishment as he looked at Jocelyn and crossed himself. "Come hai fatto a sapere che stavo pensando a mio padre?"

"He asks how you knew he was thinking of his father," said Father Giuseppe, now looking at Jocelyn as if seeing him for the first time.

Jocelyn blushed.

"He found him in the barn. His head...it was terrible."

"How you know this?"

Jocelyn shook his head. What could he say? He saw it. The driver started talking wildly and gesticulating.

"His name Giovanni. He want to know if you know who killed his father too."

Jocelyn did. Someone called Alberto. But how could he tell poor Giovanni? What would be the consequences? He shook his head. If he said nothing would it still count as a lie? The world was a thousand small shocks. They were led into the basilica, father Giuseppe now looking at Jocelyn strangely, Sister Annie smiling.

Chapter Twelve

The two men in ray bans, called Aalee and Shan, led Dizhwar to a small rented apartment in the Via Vittorio Veneto, above a shop where the sandwiches were exquisitely cut into themes, cheese and olive panini a piano keyboard, salami and cucumber a florid smiling face. Dizhwar found everything about Rome infinitely confusing. They had stopped at the Piazza Navona and the coiling serpents, men's torsos dovetailing into fish tails, stone fish heads gaping from the waters, had all reminded him of his near death experience in the toilet, and his certain knowledge that he must never sleep again.

Aalee sat opposite him and took off his glasses. One eye roved and took him in, the other remained fixed and frozen. Dizhwar wondered if, when you attained paradise, God would give you another good eye and you could throw the glass one out into the dark universe. Aalee explained that there had been a change of plan. They had discovered that each morning the Pope's private secretary and his assistant opened the papal mail in a room where the man himself ate breakfast. So rather than the enormous risks of entering the Vatican carrying explosives, they had decided to send a letter bomb. Dizhwar would have the honour of posting it.

"Will that still make me a suicide bomber?" he asked.

The glass eye seemed to swivel.

"Only if you post the letter and then kill yourself," Aalee said. "Which would be stupid."

Things moved quickly. The explosives were wrapped in foil to avoid scanning detection, then a TATP detonator was attached. It all fitted neatly in a slim envelope. Shan ceremoniously gave Dizhwar the letter, and told him how to get to the post office. Once there, Dizhwar addressed it and wrote his own name and the address of the flat on the back. He may not be a suicide bomber but at least they would know his name the moment before they all got blown to hell. He bought a stamp from a machine and dropped the deadly object in a post box. He wondered why God had singled him out to change the course of history. Everything was a mystery. He was starting to feel very tired; then his mobile phone rang. It was his Dad.

"Your mum is worried because you only took six pairs of clean pants and you said you'd be away for a week. So she wants to know what you'll do on the seventh day."

"It's alright, dad. I'll wash one of the other pairs."

"Very good. But what about drying?"

"It's like a furnace here, dad."

"But you want somewhere private. You don't want to shame your mum by having your pants on a public balcony for all the Romans to see."

Dizhwar explained that there was a small terrace in the flat where he could tie some string as a washing line.

"But you said you were staying in a hotel," said his dad.

"Ah. Hotel was full, but I met some blokes and they're letting me stay in their flat."

"Blokes? What blokes? Who are these blokes?"

"Good Moslems. They were at the airport. Just sort of hanging about and we got talking."

"And they offered for you to stay in their flat before you discovered the hotel was full? You think I'm stupid, Dizhwar?"

"Dad, I've got to go. Someone wants to use the phone."

"But you're on your bloody mobile!"

Dizhwar stopped the call. His Dad was too sharp by half.

Chapter Thirteen

The Prime Minister, Terry Bunk, had asked to see the Archbishop the morning after the disastrous broadcast. The BBC programme had gained global coverage. Samir was now a Moslem icon, his photograph adorning the bedroom walls of thousands of young men with a desire to change the world with flame and prayer. Arty had been ensconced in a private suite at the Dorchester, courtesy of the British license payer, until the corporation could decide what to do with him. He spent most waking hours trying to cash in his moment of notoriety by negotiating deals with OK and Hello magazines.

The Archbishop hadn't slept a wink and bubbles containing unwelcome words kept floating before his eyes: bummer, bum deal, shaft, pole, rod, and in another bubble: set up, tits up, cock up. Considering the previous evening had set back relations between Islam and Christianity by eight hundred years, the head of the Anglican church had been made to look a complete pillock, and the whole of the Moslem world now viewed Christianity with increased suspicion and hostility, considering all this, the Archbishop marvelled that the PM sat, feet up on the desk, smiling at a rubber plant festooned between photographs of Nelson Mandela and Elton John.

"It was an absolute disaster, and that odious little presenter made it worse," said the Archbishop.

"It got huge audiences. I mean, once word got around the pubs that there was a bit of agro. Biggest ratings pull since Lady Di's funeral," said the PM.

"It felt like my funeral. We have to do something – have another programme. A proper one. A rapprochement. "

"One that suggests we all love each other and the world is going to be a better place?"

"Well, yes. In a way. Forgive me for saying, Prime Minister, but you don't seem very perturbed by this catastrophe."

"Call me Tel. What's done is done. Now it's happened, we have to use it to our advantage, Archbishop."

"How the hell, I mean, how can we possibly use a withering attack on the very foundations of Christianity to our advantage? This could lead to war."

A shadow of something passed across the PM's face. Glory, death, apocalypse, played in the shadows of his eyes and corners of his mouth. The Archbishop shivered slightly. It was impossible to read the PM's face because his whims always outpaced his principles, to the point at which he himself could no longer remember what the latter were; consequently his face was a canvas of improvisations, manoeuvres, jockeying, with some bright and glorious personal future always just out of vision. But the Archbishop knew: something was going on here. He knew that with politicians, the worst route to information was direct questioning and often, the best thing to do was shut up and let them spin their webs in the hope they would ensnare themselves. But he was to be disappointed in this case.

"War. Please God it doesn't lead to that, but if it does...we have to deal with realities here."

"The reality that Armageddon could be triggered by a moron at the bloody BBC!" the Archbishop said. "Suddenly this thing has become a runaway horse."

"If it is, then we must make sure we ride it. How does it go in Revelation? 'And I beheld, and lo a black horse; and he that sat on him had a pair of balances in his hand.' Balances, justice."

The PM smiled. His digital watch beeped. The discussion was over. The Archbishop left the room, his mind reeling. If he had paused and looked back, he would have seen the inner door open and the familiar scuffed black shoes of Father Mack enter and the two men exchange a few words. The Archbishop sat in stony silence all the way back to Kent, then went to his study and, untempted by the pyramid of meringues before him, stared at the dull grey garden sheened by drizzle in what now passed for summer. A pile of unread dailies lay on the floor. He knew what they would say. Trouble to come. Demonstrations, recriminations, fights, terrorism, worse. What is it with these holy martyrs? He asked the solitary squirrel stealing bird food from a little table outside. What do they really want? With his heroically unscrupulous desire to help he could not understand the different, driven egotism of the martyr, how the act of annihilation created a monstrous drama of self. The Archbishop wanted to be a great man, but one loved by God and man. He did not want to be greater than God, and couldn't help feeling that by making oneself a murdering instrument of God it was an attempt to supplant him – I know His will, I am His will, I am one with Him and therefore I am Him. The martyr wanted to force the hand of life whereas he wanted to hold and lead it like the shepherd he was. In his desire to be remembered, to lead, he still retained the illusion of service, and it was going horribly wrong.

"I will never understand God's purpose," he said.

The squirrel looked inquisitively at him, then bobbed away. The Archbishop looked down at a folder marked F.A.I.T.H. containing contact details for Brother Jocelyn and Sister Annie. My children, into what monstrous region have I sent you?

Chapter Fourteen

Father Giuseppe led Jocelyn and Annie inside. Giovanni the driver remained at the entrance looking intently at Jocelyn as he entered the holy realm, hoping for a sharp renewal of faith and inspiration of purpose. The holy citadel would surely be animated by the breath of God and he could then be of use to the Archbishop and God himself. On the right was a fresco style Mary holding the dead Christ like a giant limp baby. He hadn't spoken to his own mother for over a year; faith had supplanted family. They walked around, father Giuseppe talking all the while, occasionally brushing against Sister Annie. It was a house of whispering shadows.

All eyes aspired, were drawn up by the lines of column and marble and glass, gothic longing for the unreachable, but Jocelyn's eyes, against his will and judgement, kept sliding down to the bottom of things. Embroiled serpents gaping open mouthed into a font; flat fish-like faces staring blankly out like hung-over chavs at a bus stop. A skull with clover wings below a papal painting, the black nothingness of eye sockets and nose holes. NOVI OPERA EIUS ET FIDEM – I know your works and the faith, but at the feet of Gregory XIII was a crushed and writhing dragon, heraldic device of the Boncompagni family, but to Jocelyn a serpentine reminder of the writhing life below us all.

Mostly, it was the diminutive chubby darkness of impish trolls that drew him. Were these cherubic little fatnesses meant to be angels? These diminutive soldiers in the holy pageant appeared subservient, always below, holding a cloak, propping up a parchment, but their thick curious fingers, Mongolian cheeks and cold eyes were ambassadors for disinterested chaos and presaged mayhem. Jocelyn could see the seed of Lucifer in them all. The worm turning. The servant bored with an eternal carnival of worship and obeisance. Better to be a small truculent spanner in the divine machinery than a lackey for eternity. In this toiling twine of baby fat, like glistening new born gargoyles, theirs were the faces of the dispossessed, aching for mischief, chilling in their indifference. A cherub leaning on one arm, sucking absently on his left index finger like a godless gargoyle.

It was a coiling frozen world of new horrors and frightening familiarities. Regina Christina Alexandra looked like Mrs. Peacock, his double chinned, wellington-nosed primary school teacher who terrified him into stuttering imbecility.

And everywhere an orgy of death. In the haunting corner of St. Peter's Basilica the Alexander VII monument dominated imperiously. But beneath the pomp and grandeur of the pontiff with Charity, Truth, Prudence and Justice as women staring up at him adoringly, beneath all this, in folds of drapery, was Death, the winged skeleton, creeping out like a giant bug to hold out an hour glass while Alexander prays on, oblivious to his own imminent demise. It is a cosmic joke, thought Jocelyn, the final joke that is played on us all. Then they went down to the tombs, a fat woman behind him talking loudly in a tobacco stained voice until a guard shouted "Silenzio! Questo è un luago sacro!" There, Popes Pius XI and XII in their little lit prisons of death, frozen in stone, behind glass and bars, illuminated by artificial candles.

Mostly, it was the bored cherubs indifferent to the death and misery they served that affected him, like children playing in a minefield, a syrupy thick atmosphere of marble and dull gold. The living dwarfed by the dead. Was that the purpose of these columns and pillars – to make little of our lives? We are pygmies in the architecture of faith. He felt tired of the Cross. He longed for circles, things that connected harmoniously.

How had he become a different person so quickly? What was happening to him? Sister Annie smiled at him as father Giuseppe took the opportunity of pointing at the detail of a fresco to lean in closer to her. Any closer and he'll be licking her ear, thought Jocelyn, then blushed at the thought. He had expected light and deliverance. Instead, he felt cloyed and cabin'd in this echoing mausoleum. Suddenly men appeared and whisked them away to their accommodation – the Borgia apartments.

Chapter Fifteen

The brightly lit rooms and paintings restored Jocelyn a little. They had waited outside in the courtyard by the cooling fountain, and were now ushered in by Father Giuseppe. This was the heart of the Renaissance. The blues and reds were warm and vivid, created by Pinturrichio. Here, the little, deaf, ascetic painter from the Umbrian hills, wandered and looked and planned, drew his cartoons, arranged his exquisite decorations, overlooked his army of workmen, and left a design of rich ornament. Jocelyn's knowledge of history was scanty and his knowledge of art purely instinctive, but he overheard a guide in the palace say that the paintings in these apartments used themes from medieval encyclopaedias, layering eschatological meaning and commemorating the divine origins of the Borgias. After his previous dark mood in the palace all this light and colour was welcome.

Father Giuseppe said rooms just off the main display rooms had been prepared for them and he went to supervise their bags. Jocelyn smiled at a painting of the Annunciation and felt more like himself.

"We're very privileged to be allowed in here," he said to Annie.

"Yes, Brother Jocelyn. A great privilege. Such beauty. Extraordinary to think that here was where Lucrezia was initiated into the mysteries of sex by her brother Cesare while their father, the Pontiff himself, watched and gloated as they rutted their way out of innocence. Here, where her second husband was murdered. Here, a home of incest, murder, groaning torture, sodomy, blackest plotting. Here, the pox ridden Cesare strode about in his armour recounting the tens of thousands he had hacked to bits for God and profit, mostly the latter; here the Pontiff himself clambered sweatily out of brocaded robes to father countless bastards. Here where enemies were poisoned, girls seduced and raped, illegal loot piled up. Here, where monstrous ambitions matured like tumours and the darkest of crimes were committed. What other foul deeds, despair and bloody villainy have these innocent and bright conceptions of Pintoricchio looked down upon? Fleurs du mal."

She smiled sweetly at Jocelyn, whose jaw had dropped.

"On the other hand, Brother Jocelyn, is it not possible that the Pope's people have put us here as a warning – that if we have some nefarious purpose in mind we might suffer the same fate as the Borgias' numerous victims. Or perhaps it is a Pontiff joke – to house us in this self-glorifying hall of calumny and blood to show he knows our little game? Have you ever wondered if the word 'pontificate' comes from something papist? A sort of droning on about things."

Jocelyn felt as he always did in her presence – a complete nincompoop. She squeezed his hand and his cheeks flamed. "It's all right, Brother Jocelyn. I saw you out there, disturbed by the cherubs and all that Catholic weight."

"But. It was...I mean...I just..."

"I know," she said and smiled at him. Who was this girl? A nun, but she had such outlandish notions, and she made him have thoughts about his faith that he was quite sure approached blasphemy. St. Paul would not be pleased. He felt she should be more impressed with it all. More conventional. Surely a nun should not say a word like "rutted" in the heart of the Vatican? He thought he should perhaps ask her to be mindful of her language but a large hairy hand suddenly on his shoulder shook the thought from him.

Behind them stood two unlikely looking priests in black robes with white caps. One of them was shortish, with a little pot belly, eating a cheeseburger, the other was tall and hostile. He winked at Annie, who didn't flinch, so Jocelyn blushed on her behalf. Both priests wore vicious looking swords at their waists.

"Welcome to the inner sanctum of the Vatican. I'm Father Baz and this is Father Dave. Don't be alarmed at the sight of our flamberges," he said indicating the double sided swords, "but in these dangerous times security is all. We was in the Swiss Guards, or Gardes Suisse as we say in Interlaken, before we took 'oly orders, and so 'ave special dispensation to carry blades."

"You don't sound Swiss, more Elephant and Castle," said Sister Annie.

"The Gardes Suisse is an eclectic band of brothers, Sister."

"We like to mix it up, you might say," said Father Dave.

"Point is, we're internal security for 'is 'oliness. We're a sort of pontifical hardcore, the eyes and ears of 'is 'oly presence so's 'e can pursue 'is divinely inspired musings in peace."

"Constantly watching 'is pontifical rear, you might say," said Dave, lovingly rubbing the hilt of his flamberge while he looked at Annie.

"Point is, before you can have a rabbit and pork with 'is 'oliness we need to vet you. Purely routine."

"You mean interrogate us? Like criminals," said Annie, smiling disarmingly.

Baz and Dave looked at each other and chuckled. Baz wiped some grease from his lips and gave a little belch.

"Straight to the point, eh, sister? No, more a friendly chinwag. We can't 'ave you charging in on 'is 'oliness and intiatin' some arcane discussion on ferret breeding or Kierkegaard's dialectical thinking on the teleological suspension of the ethical, now can we?"

"That would be thoroughly out of order," added Father Dave.

"So we 'ave to acquaint ourselves with the exact nature of your business," said Baz.

"So's we can put the Pontiff in the picture, as it were."

"We're here as representatives of the Archbishop of England, to learn more about current Catholic thinking, The Archbishop feels that the more ordinary worshippers, like Sister Annie and myself, can understand and forge links with your Church, the better are chances for the beginning of a new holy alliance," said Jocelyn.

"Very admirable. Complete...what's the word I'm struggling for 'ere, Father Dave?"

"Bollocks?" suggested Father Dave, and the two priests ambled away laughing and slapping each others backs, their swords swishing against their holy robes. Jocelyn looked at their retreating figures. He wondered if he was dreaming.

"I don't think he believed you, Brother Jocelyn," said Annie.

"But it's true," he replied.

"Of course it is," said Annie, smiling.

Jocelyn thought: I understand nothing.

Chapter Sixteen

The next day Dizhwar was walking in Via Luguria, trying to keep awake, when the package was delivered to the little rented apartment. He was just turning left into Via Vittorio Veneto when Shan picked up the parcel from the doormat, looked at it curiously, and walked back to the tiny kitchen, where Alee was polishing his glass eye. He popped it back in and looked with the good one at the packet. If his Italian had been better, he would have known that affrancatura insufficiente meant 'insufficient postage', but it wasn't, and he didn't. Dizhwar was just looking up at the tiny apartment window and wondering if he should tell the other two about his vow never to sleep again when Alee put a knife in the packet and slit the top open. Dizhwar was just yawning and wondering when the packet would deliver its deadly message to the Vatican when the very pavement rocked and his ears screamed as glass exploded outwards and a dazzling orange fireball cannoned from the building in front of him.

He stood and stared, his tired swollen eyes reddening and feeling the heat roll down in waves from the building. Now a moment of eerie silence, then a bank of black smoke came from the building, as if a giant was inside smoking something dark and evil and billowing out thick dark pillows of bile. He realised it all came from the apartment. It must be the army or the police. They had discovered the plot and were taking no chances. Shan and Alee never left the apartment. They must be dead. No one could survive that furnace. Then shouts, screams, alarms. People were running, others standing and staring. A woman near him wet herself and dropped her handbag. He had no idea that an explosion so changed the nature of things. He also thought – my underpants will all be burnt to ash. Mum'll be livid with me. A carabiniere on a motor bike stopped and eyed him through his helmet visor. He turned and ran.

Two hours later, the flames quenched, the building cooled with foam and water, the police entered. Everything destroyed. Two bodies charred beyond recognition. Black and smoking ruins except for a small circular glinting object embedded in the charred kitchen ceiling. A carabiniere stood on a chair and removed it with a pair of pincers. It stared at him. An eye. A glass eye. He dropped it in a forensic bag.

Dizhwar ran towards the Vatican. It seemed to be the centre of everything. He wondered what he should do now. The bomb in the Vatican would surely explode soon and he would have fulfilled his duty to Samir and to God. He was a suicide bomber who had survived. But how long could he survive without sleep? He also had no money and realised that he was hungry and thirsty. He ran over a bridge, turned left and ran straight into Death. He almost screamed.

Death nearly fell but stood his ground. His arms outstretched, white ringed bony hands, holding a black scythe in his left hand, a sinister white gaping leer on his blanched skeletal face, purple black robes folding down like priestly curtains.

Dizhwar backed away, straight into the arms of Jocelyn. They looked at each other. Jocelyn smiled.

"Amazing, these street statues. I've been watching Death for ten minutes and haven't seen him flinch, until you came along. Are you all right? You look exhausted."

He took Dizhwar to a cafe and they sat outside drinking coffee, and Dizhwar had a huge ice cream. Jocelyn told him that on first coming out of the monastery he'd found everything bewildering, but there was something about watching these street statues that calmed him – their concentration and stillness. He told him about staying in the Vatican. He didn't tell him about Annie because he knew he would blush.

"We will probably meet the Pope tomorrow," he said.

Dizhwar looked at him and a large gobbet of ice cream slid from his cone down his chest. "The Pope? But he...you really shouldn't go anywhere near him."

"Why not?"

"Well, he's an infidel. And he might have germs or something."

"But that's why we were sent here," said Jocelyn.

"But he'll be busy. He must get loads of letters. You don't want to get him all annoyed when he's opening his letters. He might be in a bad temper. Especially if it's all bills. Think how big the electric bill is for the Vatican. He'll be in a very bad mood and...and..." argument failed him. This young monk seemed OK and he didn't want him blown to hell, even though he was a Christian. Perhaps you just had to harden your heart to it all. He would try. For now, he just felt exhausted and miserable. The sound of a siren made him jump up from his seat. Suddenly he understood.

"I have to go," he said and was away before Jocelyn could say anything.

Jocelyn sat there, thinking what a strange place the world was. He had seen something in Dizhwar's eyes that disturbed him. He tried to concentrate and let it come into focus, but it refused. This ability to see into the nature of things, if that's what it was, seemed an odd gift, both absent and present, one moment there, in the shadow of a stranger, the trembling of a hand, the blink of an eye, each disclosing a story, and then it was gone and the world seemed like a flat impenetrable canvas. What was God doing? What did He want? As if to confirm this view of the strangeness of things, two pairs of eyes that had been watching him from a car with smoked windows turned to each other. Two heads nodded. They had seen enough. The car slid from the kerb like a shark in the night and stopped by Jocelyn as he stood up to leave. A back door opened and Father Baz leaned out. He smiled.

"Get in, bruv. Time for a chinwag."

Instead of going back to the Vatican Father Dave drove them along by the river, then past the Circo Massimo, along Via de San Gregorio, Celio Vibenna and straight into the Coliseum itself. Jocelyn marvelled at the perfect symmetry and scale of the building. What must it have been like? The smell of sweat and fear, fur and flesh, chestnuts, sweetmeats, slaughter of innocents, the long baying of suffering and blood in the heat of an already ancient sun. Civilization was a brutal creature indeed. St. Ignatius had come here knowing what lay in store for him – being eaten alive by wild beasts, coming here gladly with his passion for death and pain and martyrdom. He thought of the tall figure of Death again, his wide joker's smile, and how clever to have black empty eye sockets because you could project your own worst fears into their emptiness – it held the spectator. Jocelyn started as a swarthy head with a scar like lightning down one cheek, and in the full uniform of a roman centurion, plumed helmet like an additional exotic skull, opened the door and leaned in to look at him, then with a stink of cigarettes and sweat nodded at Father Baz and waved them through into the bowels of the building. What on earth is going on? Jocelyn wondered.

The car stopped and Father Dave told him to get out. He was led along a dark passage between huge stone arches. Fathers Baz and Dave walked on either side of him like guards. What had he done? What was all this about? When they were in almost complete darkness Father Baz took his arm and turned him to face a dark oak door in the wall. Father Dave opened the door. He was pushed in and the door closed. A single candle lit the room. He blinked and realised he was not alone. Someone in the corner, crying softly. His heart lurched in fear and pity. It was Sister Annie.

Chapter Seventeen

While the Archbishop waited impatiently for Father Mack to appear he tried to calm his nerves with tea and meringues. His mind was too ragged to do the Telegraph sudoku. Where was the blessed man? Always lurking and hovering when you wanted him gone, and never there when he was summoned.

How could he know that what had kept Father Mack was a clandestine meeting with the Prime Minister, a meeting which, as the PM constantly reiterated, was not taking place. In fact, he had never met or spoken to Father Mack, as he reminded him. It was the weekly report Father Mack made and this had been longer than usual, given that things were hotting up. Father Mack's reward for this betrayal was pieces of silver discretely deposited in a business bank account which only he could access, and the greater promise of Armageddon.

"Shure, he's in a roight ol' twist. Hooverin' down de meringues loike dere's no tomorrer. Shure soign he's in a twist alroight."

The PM made a cathedral of his fingers and looked out at the somnolent procession of clouds. Mack had been extremely useful: as informer, agitator, spy, scotcher of plans, thorn in the side of the

Archbishop, spoiler of good relations between the Church and Islam. He had been a useful pawn in the game of turning the Archbishop's Vision into a war cry, but now that the gears had been engaged, the cogs oiled, the wheels honed, his value was nearing an end. What to do? He wasn't sure the good Father was a man to go quietly back into the shadows. He needed a sweetener.

"Father Mack, I've greatly enjoyed these little contretemps, even though they never happened. I feel some acknowledgement is warranted for your..." here, he searched for an appropriate word, "your service, even though of course this could never be acknowledged officially."

The shit's trying to dump me, thought Father Mack.

"Perhaps, a word here, a nod there, a deanery might be offered. How would you like that?"

"I'd be preferring the loikes of a bishop," said Father Mack.

The Prime Minister smiled, but without humour. Father Mack lit a Park Drive.

"There's no smoking in here," the PM said.

Father Mack continued to puff.

"You know what a palaver it is, Father Mack. The Vacancy-in-See Committee, which takes an age to organise, then the Crown Nominations Committee, which takes a year to get quorate, and in which the Archbishops of Canterbury and York never agree anyway, then the recommendations to my office. You'll be an old man before it even got considered."

"Change 'de rules," said Father Mack, flicking his stub in the waste bin, where it continued to smoulder.

"Change five hundred years of arcane constitutional practice just to suit a whim of yours?" The PM threw his Chamomile tea into the waste bin to extinguish the small fire of cabinet papers which had now started.

"You've got a bloody war coming. Emergency powers n'all. You tell the Archbishop oim t'be Bishop next vacancy, then get 'de Queen to ratify it. Bob's your uncle. Oi'll be waitin' to hear."

Father Mack left as the fire alarms jangled their panic and the ceiling sprinklers in the PM's office started to gush, and at least a dozen security men rushed in all directions. It was always a pleasure to create confusion. For the PM things had changed drastically in the past ten minutes. More permanent measures might be called for to deal with the now troublesome priest. That was the snag with politics: someone was on your side one minute, lying and cheating and conniving like a true patriot, and the next they became Judas. It wasn't as if he asked much – just unquestioning loyal service from minions. It wasn't as if he really wanted Armageddon either – more a quick and decisive war which would give him enough time to declare a state of emergency, himself supreme Head of State, a permanent military alliance with the U.S., joint control of oil reserves in the Middle East, a permanent terrorist threat to keep people scared and powerless, and no sodding elections for at least ten years. That would ensure him several fat chapters in the history books. He would do great things, monumental things. The exact nature and manifestation of these remained a little hazy, but first things first. Father Mack. He called Head of Security on his personal line.

"Cragg?"

"Prime Minister."

"Come up now. Something special."

Chapter Eighteen

Samir was very angry. Shad made mint tea and read soothing passages from the Quoran but nothing helped. Samir walked up and down, up and down, muttering to himself. How, he asked for the hundredth time, could anyone be so stupid? The whole idea of a suicide bomber was to be with the target when you exploded the thing, or of a letter bomb to actually send it to the person you wanted to kill. Then the phone rang. Shad looked shocked, then perplexed, then incredulous. He handed the receiver to Samir.

"It's Dizhwar. He's not dead it seems."

Samir grabbed the receiver.

"I'm sorry, Father Samir. It all went wrong."

"You can say that again."

"I'm sorry, Father Samir. It all went wrong."

"I didn't mean...never mind. What happened?"

"Perhaps the infidel postal service discovered and it was a plot against us."

"And perhaps it wasn't. You posted the bomb?"

"Yes, Father Samir."

"You put the correct postage on in?"

"I don't know, Father Samir."

"Ah. As I thought. You are a cretin."

"Yes, Father Samir. What shall I do? I have no money and I have taken a vow never to sleep again and I can't understand these Italian infidels and it's so very hot and all my clean pants were firebombed and..."

"Shut up, Dizhwar. Here is what you do. Wait on the Spanish Steps near the fountain. A man will approach you. He will take you to a hotel room and there you will be given more explosives. You find a way of getting into the Vatican when a Mass is being held and you do what I sent you to do in the first place. Do you understand? It is very simple. I am deliberately making it simple for you. You, with the explosives, in the Vatican. Boom. If you do not achieve this you bring shame on me, on yourself and your family."

"But my family don't know about this," said Samir.

"It doesn't matter if they know. God knows and he will make them ashamed of you, even if they don't know the reason. How will you ever look your father in the eye again when you have brought such shame? I make myself clear?"

"Yes, Father Samir. Do you know if Arsenal won on Saturday? My dad's a big supporter."

Samir put down the receiver. There was a commotion in the outside room, then the door was pushed open and an angry looking man with grizzled grey hair entered, wearing an apron and smelling of fish, followed by an apologetic Shad.

"What is this? Who are you?" Asked Samir, in no mood to deal with another idiot.

"My name is Shan. Aasim Shan. I run a Chippy in Camden. Called Fi-Shan-Chips. It's a pun."

"Hilarious," said Samir.

"My son, Dizhwar, went to Italy on a holiday. But something stinks about it. And it's not my fish. I wanted to know if you knew something, but this simpering clod wouldn't let me in."

Shad bristled with indignation. Samir wondered if Dizhwar had been stupid enough to tell his father anything.

"Why would I?"

"I found these in his room."

He took a few crumpled news cuttings from his pocket and put them on the desk. The headlines told their own story: "Muslim Cleric Declares Day of Peace" "Moslem Spokesman in New Year's Honours List" "Moslem Cleric Takes Hard Line on Divorce", all with dignified pictures of him. Samir thought he looked a little like Omar Sharif in Lawrence of Arabia.

"I get many letters and enquiries from the young on matters of faith," he said.

"So you've had no personal contact with my Dizhwar?"

"None that I know of."

Aasim seemed to shrink. He sighed, as if the fight had suddenly left him. Only anxiety remained. His arms hung by his side like dead things. He looked up, his eyes waxy and red.

"Only, he's my boy. And his mother..." the tears welled and he gulped them back.

"Go home. Pray. God is good."

"Yes. God is good," and he left, infinitely older than when he had entered. Shad looked at Samir, in awe of his dissimulation.

"We all make sacrifices," Samir said, and returned to his correspondence, a smell of burning in his nostrils, always a smell of burning, as if a far off holocaust was coming. A forest fire. And he knew, with the certainty of a mind fully in the moment, that he would become the fire, the next lick, the next flame, the passing of something into infinity.

Chapter Nineteen

Jocelyn put an arm around Annie without thinking. She looked up at him. He thought she was probably the most beautiful thing he'd ever seen; she was a drift of flowers, and the dark, damp cell the centre of everything, the yard-stick of the universe. Then self consciousness snapped in and he blushed at his own thoughts and realised, with a small shock through his veins, that he was actually touching her.

"Did they hurt you?" He asked.

To his amazement she smiled.

"Of course not. They wouldn't dare. It's all bluff."

"But...?"

"Oh, the tears. Trick I learned from a crocodile. Completely cosmetic. I thought it might make them let me go. Never underestimate the power of tears."

"What do they want?" Jocelyn asked, deeply impressed. He wondered if she'd been taught all this in the convent.

"I'm not sure, but the less we say the more they'll tell us."

"How do you know all this stuff?"

"Because I'm intelligent."

There was no disputing that.

"Yes. Do you think we should pray? For guidance I mean."

"You can if you want. I'm going to think how we can best get out of this."

But the door opened and Fathers Baz and Dave entered. Father Baz was eating a hotdog and Father Dave was smoking a thin cigar and drinking a can of Stella. Not for the first time Jocelyn wondered about their spiritual leanings. Father Baz looked long and hard at Jocelyn.

"Listen, bruv, we're all men, and woman, of the cloth. All happily chirruping from the same hymn sheet."

"All part of God's ecstatic fam'ly, so to speak," said Father Dave.

"No secrets between God's chosen ones," said Father Baz.

"Secrets is well out of fucking order in the house of the Lord," said Father Dave.

"Which is why we brought you 'ere. To remind you of the other side of man. The carnal, brutal side. The side that's quite 'appy to string some miggle maggle arsey bastard up and let wild animals get to work on him. If you get my drift," said Baz with a smile and a small belch.

What did drift into Jocelyn's mind was the letter St Ignatius wrote when he knew what awaited him at the Coliseum, and the words tumbled out: "What a thrill I shall have from the wild beasts that are ready for me! I hope they will make short work of me. I shall coax them on to eat me up at once and not to hold off, as sometimes happens, through fear. And if they are reluctant, I shall force them to it. Forgive me — I know what is good for me. Now is the moment I am beginning to be a disciple. May nothing seen or unseen begrudge me making my way to Jesus Christ. Come fire, cross, battling with wild beasts, wrenching of bones, mangling of limbs, crushing of my whole body, cruel tortures of the devil — only let me get to Jesus Christ!... I do not want to live any more on a human plane. And so it shall be, if you want it to. Want it to, so that you will be wanted!"

This was the true embrace of Christian destiny, but perhaps a little too zealous? A tad self glorifying? He decided he would pray for guidance on this, if he ever got out alive. The other three looked at Jocelyn in amazement. Sister Annie wondered, not for the first time, if Jocelyn were not several beads short of a rosary.

"Jesus Christ, we got a masochist 'ere, Father Dave," said Father Baz.

"Bleedin' pervert more like wants to get down and dirty with poor dumb animals."

"I'm just quoting Saint Ignatius," said Jocelyn.

"Saint Ignatius my arse. Marquis de Fucking Sade more like, pardon my pigeon Latin," said Father Dave, and spat contemptuously.

"Look, for Christ's sake, what do you want?" said Sister Annie in a commanding tone that silenced the three men.

"A lady who gets down to the nub. I like it," said Father Baz, looking at her admiringly. "Tell 'em, Father Dave."

"We know. You bin mince pied ever since you left 'eathrow. You was sittin' next to a Moslem. Same bloke as was eyeballed outside when that apartment was gunpowdered, prob'ly by 'im. We reckon e's a terrorist, and you was 'obnobbin wiv 'im. So that you makes you 'ighly suspicious."

"Him?" said Annie incredulously, "But he's a simpleton, a complete nincompoop. I think he's probably mentally deficient. He got his head stuck in a toilet. He couldn't even speak properly. And you think he's a devious terrorist?"

"Takes all sorts," said Dave phlegmatically.

"See, what I'm thinking is, it was all a cunnin' subterfuge," said Baz, "and 'es a top notch terror monger. Fact that e' dispatched 'is fellow plotters with such uncompromising vigilance, suggests to me that prior to whatever other nefarious plans 'es got, 'e was making sure there's no one left to squeal."

"Cunnin' bastard," said Father Dave.

"Which brings us to you two. Hansel and Gretel. Babes in the Wood. Goodwill mission from Canterbury. Then 'obnobbin wiv a Moslem superbrain fanatic. Do me a favour perlease. Don't add up, do it? What's the game?"

Jocelyn looked baffled. Annie looked as if she wanted to laugh.

"There's no game. Is this a joke?" asked Jocelyn.

Baz gave a little belch, patted his paunch and chewed on a rennie. "Father Dave, show our young monastical friend 'ere the nature of our humour."

In a flash Dave upended Jocelyn and had him pinned upside down against the wall, and chained his ankles to a pair of rusty wall shackles. His habit fell over his face, revealing bony white knees and somewhat incongruous purple boxer shorts with prints of a sweet little white puppy dog all over.

"Maybe in a few hours when the blood's all in your noggin and you get pins and needles in your legs and feel you're gonna start losing your marbles, such as they are, then you'll have something more constructive to say," said Father Baz.

"How can you do this when you're meant to be priests?" Annie asked.

"We're on tea break," said Father Dave with a leer.

"Anyways, we're more of your Inquisitional mode. Throwbacks to a less enlightened but more 'ands on mode of papal enquiry," added Father Baz thoughtfully.

Jocelyn felt mortified, not because he was in a dungeon in the coliseum shackled upside down by two psychotic priests, but because Annie could see his puppy boxers and his skinny legs. It was horrible. He prayed for help, but none came. Fathers Baz and Dave left.

Chapter Twenty

Father Mack expected something, but not so soon. He thought the PM too much of a coward to try and harm him until all other avenues had been exhausted. It was a miscalculation. He was right that the PM was a coward, but an impatient one. Nor was he a man of great imagination, so when Special Agent Clegg left the room in no doubt as to what was required, the PM was untroubled by moral qualms or disturbing images. It was simply a problem that was being solved, thankfully by someone else. In fact, he was coo cooing at his youngest son, marvelling at the swathes of baby fat and aroma of warm bread that seemed to emanate from freshly swaddled infants, and feeling distinctly sentimental, when the black BMW followed Father Mack along Canterbury High Street, and was waiting for him as he emerged from the other side of the tower at Westgate.

The PM's wife applied a little make up beneath his eyes, and the merest dusting of powder on his cheeks to create a bronzed matt glow before he left to address a gathering of Christian luminaries at the London Missionary Society, as the BMW left the ring road and took the New Dover Road away from Canterbury. He was just rising from his chair, wearing his "Yes, I'm just an ordinary bloke" smile which really meant "I am the dog's bollocks." Just taking a sip of Evian before he started his speech and wondering what he was going to say (he hadn't had time to read it in the bullet proofed jag on the way there) when the BMW pulled into a dark field on the left and Father Mack, now with a sack tied over his head, was led from the car by two men in dark suits. He knew it was pointless to resist. He had struggled, plotted, lied and dissembled for so many long years to become a player in affairs of state and stop the Islamic apocalypse he felt sure was coming and now that it was all about to go, and he was about to go with it, he suddenly felt calmer than he had in a long time. There is a moment when some people know: this is it. The Reaper leans on the dark stile, paring his fingernails, and there is no pleading, no second chance, no point. Father Mack asked for the sack to be removed. Clegg nodded from the car. Father Mack blinked in the rainy moonlight. He was forced to his knees. A perfume of early corn, somewhere a late cow mooed, enchanting him back to his childhood, parsley and freshly cut hawthorn. Where would the sparrows nest now? Somewhere the smell of the sea. He smiled. A dull crack that startled something moving beneath the hedge. A slump forward. The heart continued to beat until the last message finally reached it. The BMW silently cruised away, black as the night.

His body was found by a farmer the next day. There were police cars, enquiries, commiserations to the Archbishop, phone calls between Church and Westminster offices. A rumour started – where?

How? Who? – and grew until it had the glittery sheen of a half truth. A phone call from someone to another someone. A radical Moslem group claimed responsibility for Father Mack's execution, people started saying. It spread like bacteria from handshake to handshake. The PM denied any such claim had been made by any group. It was scandalous, he said. The media should wait before publishing and broadcasting such unfounded stories. But by then it had attained the murky status of half truth. There's no rumour without fire. As he well knew. It was all bubbling along nicely.

The Archbishop thought it most likely that a Moslem group had murdered Father Mack, given his inflammatory remarks about Islam. You tried to keep the lid on things but it never worked. Words leaked like portholes in the Titanic. Titholes in the Botanic. Botholes in the Attic. God, I'm tired, he thought as the words rolled around in him like oily, mocking fish. His housekeeper, the shrewish Mrs. Toot entered with a cardboard box.

"This is it. His stuff," she said. "Shall I charity shop or just bin it?"

There was no family. The Archbishop realised how little he knew about Father Mack. He knew a great deal about the troublesome priest, but next to nothing about the man. It suddenly seemed all so small and sad.

"Leave his things," he said.

Mrs. Toot shrugged and put the box on the desk. The Archbishop was about to relent and ask her to take it after all; sentimentality would have to wait until this awful crisis was over, but the sight of

Father Mack's battered old bible made him stop. He took it out and perused the well thumbed pages. He came to revelation and Chapter 6 verse 5 was underscored in red biro: "And I beheld, and lo a black horse; and he that sat on him had a pair of balances in his hand." A memory tick-tocked uncertainly then flashed up. The Prime Minister. Smug. Certain. The Archbishop turned the page. Chapter 13:11 was also underscored "And I beheld another beast coming up out of the earth; and he had two horns like a lamb, and he spake as a dragon." The word 'dragon' was more heavily underlined. He turned the page and the page number 234 and the 15 of Chapter 15 were encircled and a line drawn from one to the other. Why?

He puzzled over it. Surely it was just a coincidence. The PM quoting the same scripture that was underlined in Father Mack's bible. And the other underlined verses. Why these? They shared the apocalyptic rhetoric that permeated Revelation. What was it D. H Lawrence had said? That Revelation was where the devil had slipped into the bible. It probably all meant nothing. He felt suddenly tired and put down the bible. He reached across for the Daily Telegraph and the half finished sudoku. It would calm him. It always did, the numbers flitting through his mind until a pattern was found. He started in earnest but couldn't concentrate. There was a nagging, like toothache, but what was it? He would read the funeral oratory himself. People knew he and Father Mack had their differences. It was important to show that Faith could transcend the merely personal. He looked back at the bible, opened the pages again: there was something there, something troubling. Dragon, yes, but it wasn't the word. No. The sudoku. Numbers. But what about them? Six, five, thirteen, eleven, then encircled two three four and fifteen. He could see no pattern, no logic.

He lay in bed six hours later with it still nagging. He was almost asleep as the numbers kept rolling, tombola like in his mind. He added, multiplied, sought for historical significance, symbolic meaning, but could fathom nothing. Neither could he grasp why he wanted to know. Perhaps because it was something final about Father Mack. The last mystery. His death made it seem important. Just as he was drifting off to sleep at two a.m. it came. He sat bolt upright. Eleven digits, six on one page, five on the next. Could it be? A phone number. He switched on the light, excited as a spring lamb. The five digits were probably the code, then the six the line number. He dialled 23415 651311. Nothing. Dead. He reversed the first code. 15234 651311. His heart missed a beat as he heard a ringing tone. But why? Why was this so...the call was answered. Silence. The Archbishop took a chance. He tried to change his voice.

"Dragon," he said huskily.

"Yes. Clegg? Why the hell are you phoning at this time? I'm in bed for Christ's sake!"

The Archbishop went cold. It was the Prime Minister.

"Clegg! I know it's you. There was only you and the priest on this number with the code, so what is it? What..."

The number went dead. The Archbishop sat down heavily.

"Fuck," he said quietly to no one in particular. Scenarios sped through his mind. He sifted each one, considered it, and either rejected or placed it in some provisional space in his mind. After half an hour he mentally listed the certainties. Father Mack and the PM were in cahoots over something important. The fact that Father Mack had direct access to the PM, on a number used by only one other person, confirmed that. Clegg – who was he? The Archbishop would find out. Father Mack had somehow been deceiving him, as had the PM himself. Father Mack's death suddenly seemed more suspicious.

Faith – For All In Triumphant Hope – his vision crumbled and scattered. Now his life flew apart. All its unguarded spaces revealed, open to the air. He would never be the same now; he knew that, and really, it was a blessing, for what was a vision but a fixed glare on a moving, chaotic, canvas? You create a little hopelessly implausible world inside yourself, then, foolishly, try to impose it on the world. Madness. Worse than madness. Hypocrisy. Yet he felt closer to Father Mack than he ever had in life. They were in it together now, and he would find out the truth. He put his hand on the little Bible and promised the dead man that much. Dragon indeed. He would insist on another full autopsy on Father Mack's body. Perhaps the secrets he had so jealously guarded in life he would disclose in death.

Chapter Twenty One

"Perhaps we should pray," suggested Jocelyn.

In his heart of hearts he knew the suggestion was less to initiate contact with the Creator, who seemed somewhat tardy in coming to their rescue (perhaps it really was a part of His divine plan to have them become martyrs for Christ), and more to encourage Sister Annie to close her eyes so that she wouldn't look at his skinny white legs and increasingly florid face.

"What shall we pray for, Brother Jocelyn? A crow bar? A key? An angel to lob a small explosive device so that we can get out of this?"

Not for the first time Jocelyn wondered about Sister Annie's faith. He was about to ask more when the door gave a sudden lurch. Then another. Someone on the other side cursed, and the lock began to rattle. A twist and searing of metal and the door swung open and there stood the driver, Giovanni, holding a crowbar in one hand and an Italian – English phrasebook in the other.

"Scusi. Vieni presto i miei amici," he said. "Thees way for the bathroom," he read uncertainly.

"I think our prince has come," said Sister Annie.

Giovanni got to work with the crowbar and soon had the manacles off. Jocelyn rubbed his sore ankles and his calves to get the circulation going. Then Giovanni led them through the dark tunnel where gladiators and slaves and animals from across the earth once walked, lived and died, then between two pillars and into a small area where the papal car was waiting. They got in the back and Giovanni in the driver's seat, but not before Fathers Baz and Dave, enjoying a quiet smoke in the sun, saw them and got in their BMW to give chase. They sped along the Via de San Grigorio then swung right along Circo Massimo, Giovanni jamming his foot down so the wheels screamed. The BMW was close behind and tried to touch bumpers. They came to a red light at the Ponte Palatino but Giovanni ignored it and drove across the Tiber, barely missing a bus. The BMW went around the bus and headed straight at oncoming traffic, weaving and dodging and screeching. The air was a cacophony of shouts and horns and curses. Jocelyn wondered if he hadn't been better off hanging upside down in a disgusting cell than being driven by a mad Italian seemingly intent on killing them. The only advantage was that the lurching of the car meant that every now and then Sister Annie fell against him. He could smell her hair. He knew it was all horribly sinful and promised to pray for forgiveness, but it just felt so good. And it seemed that it might be the last thing he would ever feel as the car swung right over the Ponte Garibaldi and missed crashing through the wall and into the river only by a small miracle. In the mirror Jocelyn saw the BMW lurch and swing around, then go into a tailspin and end up crashing into a row of dustbins.

Giovanni allowed himself a small smile, but kept driving. He eventually pulled off the Vale del Muro Torto by the Villa Borghese and stopped behind a van where they would not be visible from the road. He turned to look at them. The questions hung in the air – why had he helped them? How did he know where they were anyway, unless he'd been watching them? He pointed at his eyes, then at Jocelyn.

"I look you," he said.

"Gratzi," said Jocelyn.

Giovanni took out his wallet and, from it, a crumpled photograph. Jocelyn could see it was his father, the man he'd seen in his vision, or whatever it was. So that was it.

"Who?" asked Giovanni, and made is if to strike the photograph.

He owed him the information. For all Jocelyn knew this man had just saved their lives. "A man called Alberto," said Jocelyn, and faintly, for a moment, he saw the terrible moment. A hammer raining down. Dull thuds. A sickening crack, like a branch snapping.

Giovanni gasped. He seemed to age in a trice.

"Alberto. Bastard."

With a great deal of confusion, consulting of the phrasebook and hand gestures, they understood that Giovanni was going to take them to his apartment, where they could stay until they felt safe, or until Giovanni returned and could take them to the airport. First, he explained, he had something to attend to. They didn't ask what it was, but Alberto would soon be receiving a visitor. Jocelyn felt feeble. Surely he should try and stop this man from committing murder. What would it achieve? Surely forgiveness was what God wanted. But life was confusing, complicated, barbed. He decided to let things take their course. Surely if God wanted to prevent this murder, he would do so.

And so they found themselves in a 3rd floor apartment in Via Vittorio Veneto, with nothing to do but wait.

"Perhaps if we went to the Vatican again and said it's all been a terrible mistake," said Jocelyn.

"Good idea, along with stepping in front of a train, putting your head in a gas oven, and ripping off your own testicles with a rusty monkey wrench," she replied sweetly.

He gaped like a landed bloater and she went to make some tea. Annie may have been dyed in High Anglican colours, but they appeared not to have reached the bone. He looked out of the window and what he saw in the street below made him gape again.

"Sister Annie! Come quickly!" He called.

Chapter Twenty Two

Dizhwar entered the Crypt of the Capuchin Friars dazed with sleeplessness. The bodies of some three thousand, seven hundred monks and Roman poor have their bones arranged in the five rooms. In the first room, the Crypt of the Resurrection, Dizhwar looked at the multitudinous human bones arranged into a mosaic depicting Jesus commanding Lazarus to come out of the tomb. He didn't know this story, but nevertheless the ochre white stillness of the bones had a placating and restful effect on his exhausted mind. He wandered into the Crypt of the Skulls, a winged skull fashioned from shoulder blades, two capuchins in curved niches like dwarf travellers fresh back from Hades. Through the Crypt of the pelvises, the Crypt of the leg bones and the thigh bones and the Crypt of the three skeletons, the little friars stooped in their hoods, their stories long gone in this mausoleum of pretty death, both a reminder of mortality and a yearning for the infinite arrangement of things. He slumped against the wall, longing for oblivion, clutching his carrier bag full of death that he had just received from some Moslem brothers.

Annie and Jocelyn came upon him still in the same defeated position five minutes later. Jocelyn had seen him enter from the apartment window. He looked at Dizhwar's swollen-lidded, red-rimmed eyes. Behind him Annie looked at the skeletal little monks.

"All praise be yours, my Lord, for Sister Death, from whose embrace no mortal can escape. Woe to those who die in mortal sin! Happy those She finds doing your most holy will: by you, Most High, they will be crowned. St. Francis of Assisi," said Annie, looking at the exquisite arrangement of bones. "Funny how he assumes death is a woman, who kills with an embrace, whereas the holy of holies is a man. No wonder men are so violent when they are so terrified all the time."

She smiled at Jocelyn's discomfort. He turned his attention to Dizhwar.

"We're in a lot of trouble because of you," he said.

"I'm in a lot of trouble 'cos of me," said Dizhwar.

"You look exhausted," said Jocelyn.

"I must never go to sleep again. I've taken a vow," said Dizhwar.

"Why?"

"I can't remember. I'm too tired," said Dizhwar.

"They think you're some sort of terrorist," said Jocelyn.

"Not a very good one," said Dizhwar, too tired to even disguise his real purpose.

Jocelyn suddenly felt very sorry for him. He put a hand on his shoulder.

"Come with us. We've got a safe place. You can at least rest."

Annie bristled.

"Not a good idea, Brother Jocelyn," she said.

"Why not? He's exhausted," said Jocelyn.

"He's also a suspected terrorist who has got us into enormous trouble. We said we didn't know him, but how will it look now if we are seen with him? Do we really want to do this?"

Jocelyn looked at Dizhwar.

"Yes. We do."

Ten minutes later they were in the apartment giving Dizhwar coffee and cake.

"I shouldn't really be doing this," he said between mouthfuls of cake.

"Doing what?" asked Jocelyn.

"Consorting with infidels."

"But we're nice infidels."

"Doomed to roast forever in the fires of hell."

"Doesn't God love us all?"

"There is only one true God. The God of Islam. Either you accept him or you go to hell."

"You know what, Diz, when you say things like that it's as if a little tape is turned on in you. You're just mouthing the words," said Sister Annie.

"You're a woman," said Dizhwar.

"The boy's a genius," said Annie, and went off to read.

Jocelyn looked at Dizhwar and wondered how it had all come to this. Such an impasse. The truths and half truths, the downright lies, the wars and blood, the chicanery and manipulation of history.

"You're frightened," said Jocelyn.

"Scared shitless," said Dizhwar, and promptly fell asleep.

Jocelyn smiled. He opened his bag and decided to read. Anything was better than thinking. He was about to take out his little well thumbed Bible, but *The New Science* caught his eye. He took it out and opened it. He read the preface: 'Only two things are infinite, the universe and human stupidity, and I'm not sure about the former.' Albert Einstein." Chapter One was entitled 'We Are All Stardust.'

An hour later his sense of reality was unravelling yet again. Was nothing as it seemed? Was everything strange? Were all his certainties, the lights he had tried to live by, mere bubbles? He read that the physical universe was more a miracle than anything of which a religious imagination could have conceived. This world, which he had always thought of as a necessary and tawdry passage to the next, was apparently a globe of inexplicable wonders: solid objects tremble; water behaves as if alive; inanimate objects display the properties of consciousness; atoms have personalities, propensities, properties. There is a subatomic world, invisible to the eye, where everything is mysterious and unknown. He held up a hand. A universe of trembling particles. Constantly changing. Evolving. Everything is always becoming something else. He wondered how his Mum was, and saw her washing up, her hands in a cluster of shiny, popping bubbles, her eyes creased by a lifetime of smiles and worries. His Dad in the garden touching a blue rose petal tenderly, relishing its short life, looking up and smiling as the sparrows gossip and squabble, fight and love in the hedge. His heart ached to see his parents. When he got home he would call them. It had been too long. What was he protecting himself from with this long absence? The answer was simple. Feeling.

He looked up for a moment. The world is out of proportion to my thoughts. Some thoughts think themselves. It is as if my mind bleeds. And with that, an image of a small, almost dwarflike and ugly man with black bushy hair and a tangle of beard, on his way to Damascus, unshakable in his belief that things are what they seem. Then a moment, a glittering of something, a blinding, and everything is changed, utterly changed. When Annie entered fifteen minutes later she saw the difference immediately.

Chapter Twenty Three

Jocelyn turned to Annie without his usual self consciousness. No hint of a blush.

"Thirteen billion years ago our universe was a small ball, then it exploded and expanded. The earth and everything on it was originally part of some exploding star. That's what we are – stardust. Subatomic ghosts." He looked at her, both baffled and exhilarated.

"Very nice, but where's our confused terrorist?"

Jocelyn's eyes clicked from their trance. He hadn't noticed that Dizhwar was gone. He had taken his bag too. There was a letter on the table; scrawled on the front: *Please give this to my Mum and Dad. Thanks for being nice to me. Diz.* To Jocelyn's horror Annie opened the letter.

"What are you doing? That's a private letter. It's an offence to open private mail," said Jocelyn.

"For God's sake, it's also an offence to blow up people."

"True," said Jocelyn, thinking that in this new world of atoms, particles and exploding stars, the rules were probably different. Annie read it.

"Dear Mum and Dad,

By the time you get this it will probably all be over. Samir the holy priest said I had to do it and that if I failed I'd bring shame on our family even unto ten generations. So you see how it is, and I hope that you will be proud as well as a bit sad. I am quite scared and even now don't know if I can do it properly. I'm sorry I won't be able to help in the shop any more. Mum – I shall buy clean underwear. Dad, I hope Arsenal win the double and will cheer them from Paradise.

God is great.

Ever your loving son

Dizhwar"

"Shit," said Annie.

"You think he's really going to try and do it?" Asked Jocelyn.

"He seemed dumb and gullible enough."

"Let's go," said Jocelyn.

It was surprisingly easy to get into St Peters. If this was all there was to being a suicide bomber it was a doddle, Dizhwar thought, anyone could do it, passing beneath the small genitalia of some hero or saint or other, then past a few Guards who seemed indifferent to everything around them, then up the steps and through the large doors. He stopped and looked at the frescoes, the mischievous cherubs, then at the people come to gape and, perhaps, to pray. He felt sorry for them in their ignorance. He wandered, looking at the steeped clutter and defined spaces of Catholicism and suddenly felt it wasn't so different to a mosque. A lot of people looking for mystery and certainty. If Samir was right and all these souls were doomed, whose fault was that? Why were infidels created as such if they were doomed to everlasting hell? Once you started to think it became more difficult to act. Even to doubt. He sat on a chair and wept. He wanted the smell of the chippy, his Dad's scowling love and his Mum's ludicrous but safe coddling. He had no idea that his every movement was being watched intently on at least three screens by brothers Baz and Dave, in the heart of St Peter's security system, where not a mouse breathed without being photographed at least a dozen times.

"E's def'nitely 'ardwired. Look at that bulge," said Baz, squinting at the screen and focusing a close up. There was indeed a bulge beneath Dizhwar's coat.

"Why's the fucker blubbing is what I wanna know," said Dave, taking a thoughtful swig from a bottle of crème de menthe.

"These terrorists. Very emotional."

"What you reckon?"

"E's gotta want to be as close to 'is 'oliness as poss. That's what the report sez. We keep deckoing 'im 'til the cunt looks as if 'e's about to blow."

On the screen Dizhwar stood and walked towards a door.

"Go to red alert," said Baz.

Chapter Twenty Four

The Archbishop stared gloomily from his study at the sweeping rain and sooty sky. His beloved battered roses drooped and shed their petals in the misery of an English summer. He had spent a fruitless morning trying to contact Brother Jocelyn and Sister Annie. Storm clouds were gathering and, at the very least, he wanted to get them home. His last phone call, to Vatican City itself, had ended in a bizarre conversation with someone called Baz, who told him "Your little pups is well up shit creek." There was no one to turn to because he no longer had any idea whom he could trust. He even tried praying, but that made him feel worse. Perhaps he should go to Rome himself. But where to start once there? The dark, suspicious face of Father Mack kept ghosting before his eyes – whether in mockery or pleading for justice he no longer knew. He looked at the F.A.I.T.H folder on his desk with a look of disgust, then threw it in the waste basket.

Mrs. Toot entered and started dusting and pottering in apparent silence, but she had the knack of making the silence crackle with unspoken grievances. She arched her eyebrows at the folder in the basket, extracted it, gave it a gratuitous dust, then placed it back on the desk. The Archbishop bristled.

"Mrs. Toot, why do you imagine I put that folder in the waste basket?"

"I reckon you put it in 'cos you're in all of a dither and don't know what to do so you chuck one of your toys out the pram like a big baby is what I reckon."

The Archbishop's cheeks crimsoned. How dare the blessed woman be so damned right?

"I am the employer here, Mrs. Toot. If I put something in the wastepaper basket, it is then your job to dispose of it."

Mrs. Toot raised herself to her full five foot nothing.

"Technic'ly, the C of E is my employer, as it is yours, so in that respects we is equals, and as to letting someone, no names mentioned, throwing out unfinished business so he can sit 'ere all broody stuffing 'is chops with meringues 'til 'e 'as to run for the rennies, it's my Christian duty to stop 'im."

"Good God, I hope you don't speak to Mister Toot like this."

"Mister Toot is no longer with us."

The Archbishop's face fell.

"Oh, I'm so sorry, my dear woman. I didn't know. Was he taken suddenly?"

"Taken by National Express. E's gone to Bognor wiv Mrs 'Arris from number thirty two, and good riddance, I say. All 'e did was complain about 'is dodgy discs and play wiv 'is distributor cap. Let her wash is string vests, wiv 'er brassy lips an roots showing like the common plumped up bit o' fluff she is."

Words tumbled through the Archbishop's mind: fluff, muff, chuff, up the duff; plump, dump, pump, stump, frump; lips, chips, splits, tits. He blinked furiously to stop the tumult. Unaware of this maelstrom she'd set in motion Mrs. Toot was about to leave, but turned at the door and raised her duster as if about to conduct an orchestra.

"And another thing," she said.

The Archbishop waited. Mrs. Toot stood her ground, milking the moment. She waved her duster portentously.

"What is it?" He asked eventually.

"If that's electricals my name's Jimmy Tarbrush."

The Archbishop looked, and felt, confused.

"What on earth are you talking about, Mrs. Toot?"

"Them across the road. If that's electricals why aren't they parked near the electrowotsit down the road? And they're all very fine standing in the road waggling their ratchets and wotnot, but why are they all spanking new? Those ratchets is straight out of B and Q. And the uniforms – not a speck on 'em. Any electrical I seen has a creased bum and dusty knees. Electricals my Aunt Fanny is wot I say." She gave an operatic swirl of her duster, turned and was gone.

What on earth was the daft creature talking about? He left his study and went upstairs to his bedroom. The big bay window looked down on the street. Sure enough there was an electrical van and he could just see someone in profile in the driver's seat. He looked down the road and there was the mains unit. An hour later the van was still there. Why park there, unless it was to keep his house in view? Surely he wasn't being watched. What would be the point? He had no secrets. He was a public figure, the head of the Church of England, shepherd to millions. And if he was being watched, who was responsible? Terrorists? The media? Moslems? Instantly the face of the Prime Minister came to mind. Smug. Self satisfied. Feeling he was in control. Dreaming of oil and power.

He rang the local electricity board and asked what repairs or maintenance were being done in his area. None, he was told. He walked outside and approached the van. It suddenly drove away. There it was then. No one was to be trusted, including himself apparently. Was his telephone also bugged? Probably. They didn't even have to break in these days. It could be done by satellite, no doubt. Was he being watched even now? He looked around suspiciously at a ginger cat rolling on the pavement, a discarded, crushed drinks can, the grey blisters of clouds above. Nothing was innocent. Something seemed to slip in his mind so he went indoors and sat down heavily in a chair, staring straight ahead.

Less than a hundred miles away Samir left the mosque, shivered against the chill of summer and smiled. He passed Finsbury Park tube station. A pigeon hopped clumsily out of his way, its feet withered by disease and dirt. One foot had no claws, just a pinkish stump. Someone held up a Big Issue. A woman cursed into her mobile phone, "...'e like fucking told me it would never 'appen again. Even if it fucking dropped off." He registered everything without feeling connected. He had just received a text saying that Dizhwar had entered St. Peters as instructed. Soon all hell would break loose. It was coming. He felt as if he had been waiting for this day for hundreds, thousands of years. Had he walked this earth before? He saw fire, a bevel strike ancient wood, bone blackening then turning to white ash. There were still witches, evil spirits, manifest in the eyes of infidels. A secret. Something hiding. A mystery. No, not a mystery. Sorcery. Once the war had been won they would all be gone. Didn't the infidels have their own Inquisition, their own purge? This would be greater, purer, final.

Chapter Twenty Five

Jocelyn and Annie arrived at St. Peters. Jocelyn joined the queue, but Annie grabbed his hand and jostled her way though. A monk's habit and a wimple did wonders for cleaving through crowds. He wondered at the touch. How could he have thought that bones and flesh were a weary endurance until heaven was attained? Perhaps this was all there was. This could be the golden moment of his life – his hand held by a nun called Annie. Then he felt guilty for not thinking about Diz. He was his friend. Perhaps all happiness was selfish. Perhaps love itself was selfish.

They approached a Security Guard and asked for Fathers Baz and Dave. Emergencia. A call was made. They were escorted downstairs, through a labyrinth of passages. They were shown into a hi-tech room with a bank of laptops and security screens. Fathers Baz and Dave were seated. The priest who had escorted Jocelyn and Annie joined two other priests who stood by the door. One had an automatic rifle. Another had a gold ear ring and a star tattooed on the back of his left hand. Baz looked around and smiled.

"Hansel and fucking Gretel. What brings you 'ere?" He asked, thinking they must be incredibly stupid. Surely they knew what trouble they were in? Why escape and then simply turn up? They must be mental.

"Father Bazza. Look!" Said Dave, pointing a meaty finger at a screen.

There on the screen was Dizhwar in a corridor, looking around and double backing on himself. He touched his coat, where the bundle was concealed. Dave and Baz exchanged looks. Baz nodded and Dave moved towards the door.

"No!" Shouted Annie.

Brother Baz put a finger to his lips.

"He's just a bit lost, confused. You're not going to hurt him, are you?" Asked Jocelyn.

Baz narrowed his eyes. "Course not, we're men of the cloth. We're gonna send old Ali Baba there back 'ome to a land of benefits and welfare, free 'ouse and 'ave as many kids as you like. Don't bother to work 'cos some other muppet will do it while you drink mint tea and smoke your hookah. We're the good guys."

Dave left the room. Annie tried to follow but the Guard with the rifle raised it and a safety catch clicked off.

"You wouldn't shoot a nun in St Peters, would you?" She asked.

"You'd be surprised what we'd do anywhere, darlin'," said Baz, taking a thoughtful bite of a doughnut.

"I want to see the Holy Father. He wouldn't agree to this," said Jocelyn.

"You know what? I'm in a generous mood," then to one of the Guards. "Take this nob'ead to see the 'oly father."

The Guard with the tattoo took a revolver from his pocket and waved Jocelyn out of the door. Sister Annie tried to follow but a rifle barred her way.

"Just Twizzle legs, darlin'. You stay and keep me company," said Baz.

Jocelyn imagined a vast, plush room garlanded with Renaissance velvets and frescoes, but this little office was austere, a simple wooden table, and the elderly Pontificate sat in a chair smiling, as if consumed by some secret joke. He waved a hand to indicate that Jocelyn should sit. The Guard remained just behind him, the revolver under his jacket. The Pope was mechanically taking green caramelized sweets in the shapes of fruits from a box on the table and sucking them, then swallowing. Jocelyn noticed he had an enormous Adam's apple which bobbed like a fishing float in his scrawny neck when he swallowed.

"Your Holiness, this is a great honour." The Pope smiled beneficently. "It's just, my friend Dizhwar, he came here to…I mean, originally, but he's just confused and he wouldn't really…do what he was going to before…he wasn't going to do it." This wasn't going well. How could he say his friend had come to kill the Holy Father but had probably changed his mind, so they should just all forget about it and go home.

"Please. Don't hurt him."

The Pope smiled and waved his hand again.

"Your holiness, I bring good wishes and prayers from the Archbishop and he hopes there will be a deepening sense of spiritual cooperation between our two great churches."

The Pope giggled. Even to Jocelyn the words sounded forced, trite, but surely they didn't warrant outright mockery? "I've become interested in science. Apparently quantum particles are affected by the act of observation. Inanimate things behave differently when they are being watched. The universe is alive. Isn't that amazing?"

The Pope shrieked with laughter, then suddenly stopped and wiped a tear, stared fixedly at the bowl of sweets and crammed three in his mouth. With some difficulty he started talking and giggling in Italian. Jocelyn looked helplessly at the Guard, who shrugged and said:

" His Holiness he say his favourite sweet issa liquirizia, 'ow you say, the licorice. It issa good for the bowel. He also like sherbet, especially with a little lemonade to make it fizz; then he laugh ha ha ha and say he issa champagne Charlie! And the small red and yellow pips that dissolve on the tongue. They make him a very happy."

Jocelyn looked at the bright, vacant eyes of the Pope and saw a large blank canvas in dazzling white. Slowly, an invisible hand was drawing vividly coloured sweets with felt pens. He saw the old man sitting in a cave, trying to puzzle out how to get up and walk. Oh my God, he realised. This poor old buffer is completely gaga. He turned to the Guard, who smiled noncommittally. A gunshot echoed somewhere in the building. Jocelyn's stomach lurched and he ran from the room, the Guard following, the old Pope having a vague sense that someone else may have been in the room moments before the door closed. He waved a vague benedictory hand at it, then chose another sweet.

Chapter Twenty Six

Annie watches on the monitor as Baz turns into the corridor. It is like a silent film, every small flicker and gesture slowed down to photographic scrutiny. Grainy, black and white as Diz turns, looking ten years old, slightly puzzled, then, strangest of all, smiling at Baz and touching the bundle beneath his shirt. The muzzle of the revolver shining white, then a flash and silent thunder, Diz's mouth opening and eyes squeezing from the impact that lifts him clear off his feet, flips him over as the bullet hits a rib bone, then he bounces and finally comes to rest, his back arched, one leg at a peculiar angle. She runs, a Guard shouting behind her, but the sound warps into a howl and she realises it is her own voice as she turns a corner and smells blood and fire.

She is there on her knees, looking at the clammy, blue-white face and somehow Jocelyn is beside her, his face registering the horror she feels. Jocelyn takes Diz's hand. The blood pumps from his chest. The bundle he had beneath his shirt opens – it contains clean underwear, six new pairs of boxer shorts he had bought to please his mum.

"I was trying to find the exit. I just wanted to go home," Diz says, then his mouth fills with blood, his eyes flicker and he is gone, although limbs twitch and the fingers continue to grip. Jocelyn's eyes swim.

"We all want to go home," he says.

Annie takes his hand. She smiles ruefully. "Maybe he's stardust now."

A revolver prods Jocelyn in the back.

"Time to go, Twizzle," Dave whispers in his ear.

Jocelyn held Dizhwar's hand for a moment, there was something in it. His mobile phone. Unthinkingly Jocelyn put it in his pocket and followed Dave.

Baz leaned back in his chair, gave a small beery belch, and shook his head. He stared at a replay of the shooting. Jocelyn looked away. He and Annie stood before him, Father Dave and a Guard behind them.

"Fing is, 'owever you look at it, you are up shit creek without a prayer wheel."

"We've done nothing," said Annie.

Dave snorted derisively. "Nuffing 'cept cavorting wiv a bleedin' terrorist who was planning to blow 'is bleedin' 'oliness to Kingdom come. Dunnuffingmyarse."

"Terrorist? That bundle under his shirt was clean underwear," said Jocelyn.

Dave shifted uneasily. "Bleedin' terrorists put explosives anywhere these days. Incendiary pants wouldn't put it past 'em."

"We was taking necessary precautions to protect the 'oly father, an' our task was made a lot bloody 'arder by you two muffins poking your tits in," said Baz.

Jocelyn could feel shock waves pulsing through his body, a nausea that seemed to fill every cell. Baz was saying something about being in a difficult position, about ecumenical niceties, the need to ferret he and Annie away until a solution could be found.

"You mean you're going to drive us somewhere, then have us shot and blame some Islamic group," said Annie

"Tut tut. Just like a nun. Always look on the dark side. We need you out the way for a bit is all. The news will break in about an hour. Already the Papal PR retinue will be sharpenin' its pencils and getting' the right angle. You're a bit of a spanner in the works." He nodded to Dave, who prodded Annie and Jocelyn out of the room. They went down a corridor, through a tiny security door, down some dank steps that, surprisingly, smelled of the sea, and into an underground car park. Security Guards buzzed everywhere. The air was charged with something impending.

"Why on earth did he come to St. Peters?" Annie asked.

"Maybe just to see it," said Jocelyn. "He wasn't that bright. But neither was he a murderer. It's all so disgusting. Everything."

She looked at him.

"Some things…"

"What?"

"Nothing."

"They're going to kill us, aren't they?"

"Yes."

A Mercedes was suddenly there. The back door opened and Annie and Jocelyn got inside. Baz got in front with the driver. The car cruised up a ramp, a security gate folded up in the roof and they were out in the blaze and glare of Via Della Conciliazion speeding along to God knows what. Jocelyn felt in his pocket and there was the letter Diz had given him to send to his parents. He felt an overwhelming weary urge to cry until he was exhausted, and then sleep forever. Which is what he would be doing soon, he supposed. They turned into a side street. A baker's van in front of them suddenly braked. The driver cursed and almost hit the van. He looked behind but there was a car close to them. He honked his horn and swore. The van suddenly revved and reversed quickly into the Mercedes, taking everyone by surprise. Baz's head jerked back painfully. The driver opened the door and strode towards the van, already reaching for a gun. The passenger door flew open and smacked him in the face and he fell to the pavement. Baz had recovered, but the passenger door was opened and Giovanni leaned in and took the gun. He shook his head at the groggy Baz.

"Mi scusi, Padre." Then, to Annie and Jocelyn, "Quick. Issa not much time before all hell issa comings and goings." He smiled at

Jocelyn and drew an imaginary blade across his own throat. "Bastardo Alberto kaput. Grazie."

They got out of the Mercedes and into the waiting car behind them. Giovanni put it into gear. Jocelyn suddenly remembered something. He got out again. Giovanni shouted at him. Annie shouted, but he ran back to the Mercedes. Where was it? There on the floor. Mr and Mrs ABDALLA, 12 Templar Rd. He picked it up and reeled as Baz leaned over and hit him from the front seat. He felt his cheek explode. Then a hot rod of anger sparked through him, such as he had never experienced before. His hands flashed out and locked around Baz's throat, surprising both of them. He squeezed. Baz's nails bit deep into Jocelyn's hands but he felt no pain, just the wild unleashing of anger. He squeezed tighter and Baz's face went pink, then one of his eyes distended – he could see broken veins. Did God make this moment or was it waiting to happen from the moment the universe crashed into being? Did it matter? A sandpapery rasp came from somewhere inside Baz. Jocelyn was aware of horns honking, of the little Fiat speeding past them, Annie's fearful face in the back, then police cars and papal Mercedes stopping behind him. He released Baz, got out of the car and ran. A gun fired and a window broke by his head. Another shot ripped into a parked car. He turned into a shop and ran inside, a small startled man sitting among hams and cheeses watched him race through to the back, into a little kitchen where an elderly woman was rinsing her false teeth under an old copper tap, out into a small yard. He clambered over a wall and through another shop, smelling of mothballs and incense, rolls of cloths in reds and greens and oranges piled high, out again into the street, across and down an alley that ended in a small public garden, with houses beyond it. He caught his breath and touched his bloody cheekbone. The sweat poured from him. I must get rid of this habit, he thought. He looked around. Washing was drying in one of the gardens. Five minutes later a new Jocelyn squeezed through the fence of the garden, wearing baggy black trousers, a workman's white shirt and a red scarf, his habit left neatly on the ground. He had his wallet containing seventy three euros and the letter to Diz's parents.

Chapter Twenty Seven

He had to be strong for her sake. He had a great need for tears, but they would have to wait. For her sake. A hunger for revenge. That would wait too. For now, only she mattered, and he realised how much he loved her. It was never said, but it was palpable, a solid thing in the heart, real in the cold hand of grief. As usual, she was there before him. Always quicker of mind and heart. He hadn't even heard her enter the room. He put down the phone gently.

"Dizhwar?" She asked.

He nodded. They had known each other so long. She read everything in his eyes. Quietly she left the room to prepare the evening meal. Moments later he heard the crash as she fell to the floor.

After he made the call Jocelyn felt a need to do something different. He had promised to keep the letter and give it to them personally when, if, he got back to England. He walked around the …district, keeping his head down if he saw a new Mercedes or a police car, until he found himself in a narrow cobbled street. It was early evening. A chill was beginning to mist windows. Diz was dead, his body already becoming something else. Ahead of him he saw the tall figure of Death walking towards him and turn in a doorway. Jocelyn followed. It was a bar, full of shadows and creosoted wood. A low ceiling and the only small window, by the door, made it dark. An ebony, scratched bar ran the length of the room, and behind it a forlorn looking one armed man was wiping the top with a filthy cloth. It was ideal.

He ordered an absinthe, without even knowing what it was. The first taste was sharp, acrid, burning. Death sat in a corner, drinking off the dust of a long day. A silver cowboy had a beer and a plate of pastrami, his gun resting beside the plate. Two centurions sat smoking and drinking rough red wine, counting out piles of euros, while other street statues relaxed and smoked and drank. They took in Jocelyn without interest. He sat at the bar and sipped his drink. Its unfamiliar warmth started to settle inside him and he ordered a second. He was about to pay when a few euros were thrown down for the barman.

"On me," said a nondescript voice, somehow weary beyond years. He hadn't noticed the pale, small man beside him, a few strands of exhausted hair like thin rope over his mottled dome. he spoke English but with an accent Jocelyn couldn't place, There was something ancient and lizard-like in its rasp,

"Thanks. Who are you meant to be?" Jocelyn asked.

The old man shrugged indifferently. There was something unwholesome about his waxy face and old clothes. Jocelyn suspected it was a few days since he'd washed. The old man took out a filthy rag and spat into it, then sipped his brandy.

"I've lost my friend, a girl that…I liked, people want to kill me, and my faith is in tatters," Jocelyn said, almost to himself. The old man took out the rag and spat into it again, examined the phlegmy mucus, and returned it to his pocket. He smells like dead meat, Jocelyn thought.

"All love is tragic," said the old man. Jocelyn turned to him. "Someone dies, or leaves, or gets ill and their brains turn to jelly. Love can only end tragically."

With that cheerful thought, Jocelyn gulped down his drink.

"Are you a poet or something?" He asked.

"No, I'm a filthy old man who has no illusions left. I've done terrible things, and the idiots never minded. People are all stupid fuckers. They believe anything just because some dickhead tells them to."

"Who are you?" Jocelyn asked.

"Now? Or before?" The old man wheezed and hawked up another gobbet of something disgusting.

"I don't know. Both."

"I told, you, I'm just a filthy old man. I used to be God. A long time ago."

Jocelyn looked at the withered, decrepit little figure and smiled.

"God. The God? The Almighty. The one and only, holy of holies God."

"Yup," said God, and lit a cigarette to put between brownish crooked teeth.

"I don't believe you," said Jocelyn.

"No one did. That's why I got fed up with the job. Waste of bloody time."

"So I've given the whole of my adult life so far to worshipping and praying to you. Do you think I'm a complete fool?"

"Yup," said God.

"Prove it. Give me a sign," said Jocelyn.

God sighed. "Everyone wants a sign." He slapped his hand down hard on the bar top, then lifted it. A fly was squashed into a little yellow and red pulp. He scraped up the mess with a matchstick, put it in his hand, closed his fist and blew into it, then opened his hand. The fly glistened, alive and re-energized, and then flew away. "That fly will now live for three hundred and twenty seven years; in twenty years time it will feed on the remains of an assassinated American president. In fifty years it will fly into the eye of an astronaut, who will consequently suffer from a mild infection, enough to make a mistake in his calculations and fly too close to the sun. His ship will evaporate. Cause and effect. Miracle and disaster. Whole bloody cycle goes on and on."

"Jesus Christ," said Jocelyn.

"Don't start me on him."

"You're some sort of conman," said Jocelyn.

"The ultimate."

"Give me another sign."

Wearily God closed his eyes and concentrated, then opened them.

"I've just caused an earthquake in new Mexico." He looked at the barman, who flipped on a small TV. CNN news was suddenly interrupted and the Announcer said that reports were coming in about an earthquake in New Mexico.

" Sixty confirmed fatalities so far," said God.

"Sixty confirmed fatalities so far," said the Announcer.

The barman switched off the TV.

"Oh hell!" Said Jocelyn.

"Don't get me started," said God.

"But you've just caused sixty deaths to prove a point," said Jocelyn.

"No, you've just caused sixty deaths to prove a point. If you hadn't walked into this bar, it wouldn't have happened."

It was ridiculous. "If you're God, then you're God forever. You're eternal. Alpha and Omega. You can't suddenly stop being God."

"Yes, I can."

"How?"

"I'm an atheist. I don't believe in myself. I just think I'm a filthy old fucker who causes mayhem when arseholes like you insist on being given a sign." He turned to Jocelyn and for the first time looked him in the eyes. "Look, damn you!" He said. Jocelyn looked into the muddy, slightly jaundiced eyes. It was like a jolt of electricity. Landscapes of dark pain and jagged feeling, wildernesses beyond reason, explosions of life into nothingness. This crowded and lonely old man carried the ancient of days in him. No wonder he looked terrible and drank so much.

"So you've just given up?" Asked Jocelyn.

"Not before time," said God, and spat again into the rag. He ordered another brandy. "Human race – stupid little experiment I should have ditched years ago."

"But I'm supposed to be a Monk. What do I do now?"

"My advice, get drunk, get laid, then shoot yourself in the head."

"Thanks."

"My pleasure."

"There's something else I want to know. If sex is so wrong why is the whole world at it like rabbits?"

"Just my little joke. I had no idea the dozy sods would take it all so seriously. I mean, it's such a ridiculous activity. Oh oh oh I love you oh now I don't love you oh oh now I love myself…! Squish squash splish splosh. How can the dozy fuckers not see the joke?" His little raspy moan skittered off into a coughing fit and another hearty spit into the rag.

Jocelyn asked about the fly. Why would it live exactly three hundred and twenty seven years. He had a vague sense of unease about it. God chuckled wheezily.

"That's all everything's got. Then it's finito for homo sapien. Goodbye and good night."

"How will it end?"

"You don't want to know." He was probably right. And somehow it didn't matter. Atoms, particles, stardust, black holes, universes disappearing, new ones being born. There was so much beyond the merely human. He turned to tell God how much life had changed for him in the past few days, but he'd gone. All that was left was a smouldering cigarette butt in the ashtray.

"Where is he?" He asked the barman, who shrugged, looked up at the stained ceiling, and emptied the ashtray.

He had one more absinthe, and walked out into the night. He would find the British Embassy. He would get home. He trusted Giovanni would do the same for Annie.

Chapter Twenty Eight

It was three days later and Jocelyn sat in the tiny living room above the chippy at 12 Templar Road. Below a small queue was forming, wondering why Mr Abdalla, ever reliable, hadn't opened. A buzz started. Didn't you see the news? The boy Dizzy was that terrorist who tried to blow up the Pope. Always thought he was cracked. Must run in the family. What are they planning next? His chips were always too greasy anyway – probably fried in bomb oil. The chippy's days were numbered.

Mrs Abdalla read the note for the fifth time, as if holding the paper and savouring the words would bring back her son. Mr Abdalla kept blinking and rubbed his calloused hands together.

"I didn't know him long, but we became friends. He spoke about you. I think he loved you very much," said Jocelyn.

"And what bloody use is love when it can't stop your boy being shot?" Mr Abdalla said. "Dizzy, son, why couldn't you become an Arsenal supporter instead of a bloody terrorist? God knows there's enough tragedy at the Emirates these days for anyone. Why couldn't you bloody stop him?" He turned on Jocelyn.

"Hush, father. This young man is being kind. Coming here."

"I know, I know…I just…" Mr Abdalla's words trailed off into two large amulet tears that rolled down his craggy cheek. He needed to blame someone. "That bloody priest, filling his head with all sorts of bollock nonsense."

"I think Dizzy was a bit confused and they took advantage of him," said Jocelyn.

"I bloody tell you – that priest. When I get my bloody hands round his bloody neck he'll wish himself in hell."

"All in good time, father," said Mrs Abdalla, then to Jocelyn, "You know, they won't let us have his body. They say it's evidence or some such foolishness. We can't say goodbye."

"I'm so sorry," said Jocelyn.

There was nothing left to say. He turned to leave, then remembered.

He took Dizhwar's mobile phone from his pocket and put it on the dresser, next to a photograph of Dizhwar as a little boy in an Arsenal shirt. Then he left them to their grief.

Given that they had been at the centre of an international incident Jocelyn and Annie were summoned to Downing Street for a debriefing. The PM's office had arranged for Jocelyn to stay at the Dorchester Hotel that night, then meet the PM the next morning. Jocelyn had been hugely relieved to know that Annie was back safely, presumably back at her convent for now. He sat in the hotel room wondering what to do with the rest of his life, when the phone rang.

"How are you?" She asked.

"Sister Annie! Where are you?"

"Next door."

He was aware of the Security Guards strategically placed along the corridor. One of them smirked as he knocked on her door. She touched his arm as he entered and he wanted her hand to stay there forever. They stood awkwardly – there were so many things to say about what had happened in Rome that it seemed easier to skirt them and talk about now – the meeting tomorrow, how strange it all seemed. Something had changed between them. An electric calm held them.

"What now, Jocelyn?"

"What do you mean?"

"The way you're looking at me."

"I'm thinking – you are the sunlight on fields of corn, you are the still space in a storm, the reflection of the moon on night waters, the secret of flowers, the..."

"Why don't you just shut up and get naked?"

He gulped.

"But you've taken a vow of chastity."

"I kept my fingers crossed."

"I don't know what to say."

"Thank God for that."

"I don't think I will. I met him and I wasn't impressed."

"Then come to bed."

It seemed an excellent idea. Half an hour later he knew it was the most excellent idea ever in the history of the world. An hour later she lay in the crook of his arm and he watched a moth outside flitting against the window. Out there was another framework altogether – the elaborate and ornate machinery of life, much of which seemed to consist of ways for people to cheat other people. He wanted to stay in this room forever. With her. Sister Annie. Annie.

Chapter Twenty Nine

Terry Bunk was feeling pleased. He loved it when things didn't go according to plan, but one better. The plot to destroy the Vatican and the heroic thwarting of the terrorist by Catholic priests gave a whole new slant to the situation. He looked in his office mirror, angled to allow for the most flattering light to reflect him back to himself, straightened his tie and gave that boyish, slightly cheeky, wide smile that people loved. Good Old Terry, he said, and winked. Things could swing whichever way he wanted now. Not he, exactly, the U.S. President of course, it was what he wanted that counted, but good old Terry would be lapping up the crumbs behind. Photo shoots at Camp David, the White House lawn, shirtsleeves rolled up and addressing the troops in – well, in wherever they decided to invade next. Anywhere where there was oil really, or the big one – Iran. And at home – that would be a shot in the right direction too. Increased powers of detention, on constant terror alert, from orange up to red, pop down to yellow, then shoot back to red. Take it down from red to avoid overkill. Everyone anxious. Need for vigilance. Neighbourhood Watch could become just that. No one was safe. Everyone a potential enemy. Excellent. His personal power base would be enhanced, as would his personal stature and, more importantly, the history books could be written while he was still in office – the man who took on Islam. He wondered who would play him in the film. They'd need a new sort of heroic actor, a cross between Olivier, Connery and Gielgud, with a soupcon of rock and roll – a young Jagger in full sexy serpent mode. Character, strength, charm, a good riff and gravitas. Terry did a little rock and roll shuffle and pout at the mirror. Good old Carol was up the duff again, so a lot more press coverage there. If they could time the birth with military victory in – wherever it was, that would be a double coup. Time Magazine, Hello and OK. Newsnight specials. He might even make an album. Powerful songs with meaningful lyrics, about loss and courage in adversity, the merest whiff of Christianity to give them depth. Christ, he hadn't learnt to play guitar just to keep his bloody kids amused at bedtime. By the time he left office the old Bunker coffers would be bursting at the seams with loot.

His PA buzzed through. "They're here, Prime Minister." Already? God, how time flies when you're enjoying yourself.

The Archbishop was shown in, followed by Sister Annie and Brother Jocelyn. Terry registered the bloom on Annie's cheeks. He shook hands warmly with each of them, careful to make meaningful eye contact, the hint of a smile behind his sympathetic We're in this together look. They sat in leather backed, studded chairs. Terry went to the window and looked down at the security guards, the police, the wet pavements glistening with sky. Westminster light shone on him. His light. He turned.

"This situation is deadly serious, but then you know that."

No one spoke.

"This was clearly an organised attempt to blow up the Vatican, linked to terrorist networks all over the globe. That's what Intelligence is telling us. Possible planning networks in Syria and Iran. We can't stand by and do nothing. I've had the President of the United States on the phone this very morning, suggesting possible actions. Now, Brother Jocelyn and, er…Sister Annie, as actors in the Vatican drama you will have to be properly debriefed after this meeting. Then we want you to help us, entirely informally of course, and of your own volition, to publicly condemn the cowardly violence of these terrorists. This would greatly assist our efforts to create the right kind of attitude – sad but robust. I'm sure your Christian principles have been greatly offended by this action, as have mine." He waited. This was usually when people nodded and muttered their agreement. It wasn't happening for some reason. The Archbishop looked like a hunted man. He was completely absorbed in examining the switch of a lamp for some reason. Jocelyn just looked ahead, a slight smile on his face.

"Whether the Catholic or Protestant church, it makes no difference. Your Christian principles, like mine, have been affronted. Brother Jocelyn?"

Jocelyn seemed to come out of a trance.

"Which principles would these be, Prime Minister? The ones that shoot a young man armed only with six pairs of underpants. Or the ones that just want any old excuse to go looking for a fight? Or ones that you're about to make up?"

Terry gaped like a fish for a second or two, then smiled, stepped purposefully and clapped Jocelyn on the back. "Sense of humour. Irony. Joke in adversity. Spirit of the nation. Churchillian. Black humour to lighten the moment, no offence to our multicultural beliefs and convictions. God likes a sense of the ridiculous."

"Perhaps that's why he chose you as Prime Minister," said Jocelyn. In some background room of his mind he couldn't believe he was saying all this, but in many other rooms he knew he was utterly transformed. A night with Annie. He could still feel her breath as she slept.

"Brother Jocelyn, I remind you of your calling. You were chosen precisely because of the depth of your faith. That faith is now being called to action. England expects. I expect. God expects."

"Oh, him. I met him. Wasn't that impressed. I find the New Science more interesting now. Atoms and stuff. And other things," with a quick look at Annie, which did not escape Terry's lizard eyes.

The Archbishop was switching the lamp on and off.

"You won't find God by looking through a microscope. You'll find him in your heart. Atoms can't give you redemption."

"I don't want redemption. You can stuff it."

"Archbishop, aren't you going to say something? And why the hell are you fiddling with that blasted lamp."

The Archbishop looked up, startled.

"I was just wondering – is this lamp buggered? I mean dugged? Bugged?"

Terry gaped at him. What the bloody hell was going on?

"What are you talking about? This is my office. Nothing's bugged." Of course it was, but that wasn't the point. The Archbishop looked around fearfully. Nothing was innocent. Everything was watching everything else. Everything was listening in. He went to the mirror and saw a haunted face staring back at him.

"Who's there? Is this a two way mirror? Who is watching on the other side? Hello!" He shouted. He picked up a photograph of Carol, smiling like a lumpen china doll, a new baby in her arms. "Is this picture recording us?" He picked up a glass paperweight (gift from the Emperor of Japan) and smashed it down on the photograph. Terry was already pressing the emergency button under his desk. The Archbishop was on his knees, lifting the carpet to see what was hidden beneath. The door burst open and two dark suited men rushed in, revolvers cocked and ready.

"It's alright," said Jocelyn, and went to the bemused and cowering Archbishop. He touched his shoulder and felt, seemed to see, a small shivering white thing in a corner, the walls and ceiling spiked with dark and vicious looking instruments. He turned to the PM. "He's ill. Tell them to put their stupid toys away. Call an ambulance."

Terry nodded to the Security men, who holstered their guns. The Archbishop looked up pitifully at Jocelyn. He seemed to be searching his mind and finding only confusion and jumble.

"I had a thing, a plant thing. A fanny. A fan. No. What is it?"

"A plan. You had a plan, Archbishop," said Jocelyn.

The Archbishop's eyes lit up. "Yes, yes, a plan. What was it? Prat. Fat. Fart."

"Faith. It was called Faith."

"That's the one," said the Archbishop happily, and sucked his thumb. Terry waved a finger around his forehead to indicate the Archbishop had taken leave of his senses and the two Security Guards gently led him out. Terry's smile had vanished.

"Right. Enough fannying around. I've had a statement drafted and you are going to read it at a world press conference this afternoon." He gave Jocelyn a piece of paper, who quickly scanned it. "…fear for our lives at the hands of this cowardly murderer…all decent people at risk…regrettable…need for firm government…righteous punishment…God is loving but demands justice…I'm not reading this."

"Oh yes you bloody are. It's what you believe."

"It's bollocks."

"Jesus, you've come out of your wormhole, haven't you? Brother. You will read it, otherwise there will be consequences."

"For example?"

Terry took a DVD from his desk drawer and put it in a machine. Moments later the screen showed Annie and Jocelyn in bed in a passionate encounter. "It goes on for quite a while. Either you co-operate or this mysteriously finds its way to various newspapers today. It's even more interesting with sound."

"You bastard. I never dreamed you'd do anything like this," said Annie.

"You took one for the team, Annie. Photo op too good to miss. Now tell this muppet to co-operate."

Jocelyn looked at Annie. What was going on?

"Jocelyn, I'm sorry," she said.

"I don't understand." They stared at each other.

"Oh, for heaven's sake, work it out, man. She was a plant. She works for me. We knew that with a bit of fluttery eye stuff the Archbishop would choose her. You going all goggle eyed over her was a bonus." Terry looked at his Rolex. "We don't have time for this crap. A de-briefing then you read what I gave you."

Jocelyn, his heart a cold dead thing in his chest, left the room. He slammed the door shut and turned, straight into the arms of Father Dave, now wearing a dark suit. Baz stood behind him, wearing a bandage around his neck. His right eye was still very inflamed and his voice hoarse. He touched his throat involuntarily and gave a small smile at Jocelyn.

"Hello, bruv. Small world, eh. Let's go quietly, shall we? Unfinished biz."

Inside Annie was furious.

"Good job, Annie. Amazing really."

"I had no idea it was a Terrorist thing. You said just monitoring. Opinion. How the wind was blowing," said Annie.

"Nothing happened, did it? It's all working out brilliantly, except we've now got Loony Tunes as an Archbishop. Didn't see that coming," said Terry with an ironic smile. "But might work to our advantage. Archbishop has breakdown – the burden of an Islamic global threat type of thing. I could hug him in the Nursing Home."

"You bastard. You snivelling little rat. Is there nothing you won't do to further the career of Terry Bunk?"

"Oh my God, you actually like the monk, don't you?" said Terry gleefully.

"Yes. He's decent. And he cares for me."

"I wonder if he'll care so much if he knew some of the dodgy things you're been up to while in the employ of this high office?"

Annie's face darkened.

"Look," Terry always prefaced a remark with "Look" when he was about to make a serious moral or emotional point. "If anyone has respect for love, romance, caring, it's me, but we have to balance that with a very real threat to our lives, our beliefs and way of life…"

"Don't make a fucking speech at me, you sanctimonious cunt!" said Annie, and turned to the door.

"OK, you've just talked yourself out of a hundred and fifty grand a year job, but if you think you can make a pile more by dishing dirt to the press I'll have you in a high security prison, for reasons of national security, for the rest of your life, or worse, quicker than you can take your knickers off for Holy Joe."

"Terry, when you die they'll have to bury you on the moon just to stop the smell spreading. You're a disgrace to the human race." She was gone. Terry felt slightly ruffled, but a good set to always made him feel frisky. Where was bloody Carol when he wanted her?

Chapter Thirty

Jocelyn sat in the chair facing Dave. It was a small room somewhere in an underground chamber in Whitehall. No one had said he was a prisoner, but that was exactly what he was, although all he could think of was Annie. How she had betrayed him. How can anyone be so physically intimate while carrying such dirty secrets in their heart?

"Luv. Mucky business. What was it Shakerags called it – this pleasant madness?" said Baz.

"And that uvver one. Wassisname? Johnny Crush. Burning ring of fire or something. Sounds more like diorreah to me."

"Shut the fuck up, Dave."

"Right."

"OK, Bonzo. It's very simple. You read out what the PM gave you, then you're a free man. Refuse, and it's your nuts in a vice. Go to the press and your dear old mum will receive a pot of ashes wiv your moniker on. Simple choice."

"Dead simple, if you'll excuse the pun," said Dave, who was starting to annoy Baz.

"So how come you two are priests in the Vatican one day and thugs in London the next."

"'E works in mysterious ways."

"You were plants. Sort of double agents," said Jocelyn.

"We can be fucking quadruple in the service of our country if we 'ave to," said Baz, and took a bite of a mushroom slice.

"Quintet. Sextuplet if needs must," added Dave unnecessarily.

"So, Friar Tuck, you gonna be a good boy or do we 'ave to waste our time persuadin' you."

"On one condition," said Jocelyn. If Samir's parents could have their son's body back so they could give him a proper funeral, he'd do it, he said.

Baz made a call on his blackberry, listened, then put it on hold.

"No way. They gotta do a proper postmortem and enquiry," he said.

"Then you can stuff your news conference," said Jocelyn.

Baz consulted some more.

"In a magnanimous gesture of multicultural 'ands across the water all light a candle for peace n' understandin' and we're all one big 'appy fuckin' global family bollocks, the PM hisself has agreed that the family can 'ave a decko at the croaked Mustapha, in a dignified and befitting manner, despite the fact 'es a bleedin' murderin' bastard."

"He didn't murder anyone. You shot him, if you remember."

"Jus' give me an answer before I ask Dave 'ere to introduce you to the delights of persuasive interrogation."

It was something. They could see their son. The big questions of the world, truth and reality seemed to shrink in the face of one small act he could make possible. He had been betrayed, by everyone, but he could do something for Diz.

"What the hell. I'll do it," he said.

"Bingo," said Baz into his Blackberry.

There was a great deal of backstage manipulation during the next few hours, as if the News Conference was a giant theatrical spectacle, which is exactly how the PM liked to think of it. He'd insisted that the Archbishop be seated next to him, and afterwards, when it was announced that he was a sick man in the first stages of dementia, this would be seen as a gesture of profound sympathy by the PM. Annie had agreed to be on the platform, with a promise that if she did so, she would receive a payoff of two hundred thousand pounds in advance, and be left alone for the rest of her days. It'll all come out great, Terry said to himself in the mirror. He'd had a quickie with Carol in the kitchen, up against the metallic Frigidaire, and this had given his cheeks a bit of colour. He looked relaxed and handsome. If anything, the streak of grey on either temple was an improvement – a sign of the strains of office, but of statesmanlike confidence. And bloody sexy.

"Now, we're ready to rock, you good looking son of a gun," he said to himself, and lifted a smoking gun finger to his lips.

Chapter Thirty One

The room was full. The air alive with expectation. Seasoned journalists speculated on how the tone would be managed by the PM and his PR team: gung ho warmongering? Resolute iron fist talk? Revenge and compassion gooily spooned together? What they were already betting against was calm diplomacy and rational thought. That wasn't Bunk's style. A former American President, in a lucid moment free of sexual intrigue, once advocated caution: "You can always wait and kill someone next week, but you can't bring them back next week." Bunk's view was more that if you killed someone this week you could always kill someone else next week, except that you didn't actually go and kill them yourself. That would be silly, and dangerous. You had armies and mercenaries and people to do that stuff for you, of course. You took off your jacket and rolled up your sleeves for the cameras, but that was about as close to the action as Bunk ever got. He wasn't stupid.

There was a buzz of side betting on the euphemisms Bunk would use for taking Britain to war again: 'humanitarian intervention' was three to one, 'making the world a safer place' five to two and 'ridding the world of evil' came in at six to two. Andy Cope of the

Daily Star suggested 'Let's Shaft the Shits' but there were no takers. Bazza Gripe of the Telegraph suggested 'In order to defend our values of freedom and democracy I am prepared to fight to the last drop of someone else's blood,' but this just received a laugh. What they did know was that the Terry Bunk warmobile was about to hit the road again, with Terry heroically leading from the rear. Some of the journos had grown reluctantly fond of him over the years – his ineluctable self-aggrandising, phoney chumminess, immense self-entrancement, personal greed, unforgiving vanity – these had defined the political landscape for years now, and they would miss it.

Bunk strode in purposefully and the flashbulbs started popping. He'd really gone to town with the pancake make-up, suggesting that the tone might be film star/dashing hero about to heroically defend the nation. He sat spotlight centre on a slightly elevated chair, the Archbishop to his right and next to him Annie. To his left Jocelyn and Hersham 'Sausage' Malone, the Minister for Foreign Affairs, so called because a former mistress compared his manhood unfavourably with a cocktail sausage. In private his wife said that was being over generous and that 'Caterpillar' Malone was more appropriate. The joke followed him around the corridors of power to the extent that he developed a nervous tic below his left eye, which twitched uncontrollably whenever anyone laughed, as he assumed it was at his expense. He once punched the Home Secretary on the nose during a cabinet meeting when he smiled to himself over some private recollection. Malone was made to apologise, which he did bitterly and resentfully, and that evening Oscar the family cat was startled to find himself booted into the garden for purring during News at Ten. Malone stared miserably ahead, wondering which one of those bastard journalists would sneak in a 'sausage' reference. Perhaps if he kept quiet he'd avoid another public ridicule, after all if he didn't say anything there'd be nothing to quote, but this made him more miserable because he liked airing his opinions at great length in public. That was his job, after all.

Terry looked at his PA and a hush filled the room. Baz and Dave moved silently behind him. The PM narrowed his eyes and looked around the room, then smiled ruefully as if bearing the moral weight of the world on his designer clad shoulders. He looked sadly at the Archbishop, who appeared to be engrossed by a shaft of light across the floor in front of him. He frowned, puzzled by something about it, and moved his head to change the angle. Annie glanced across at Jocelyn, but he stared ahead, resigned and miserable. Everything was over.

"I've called this press conference because we have just experienced one of the most savage and unprovoked attacks on much that we hold sacred. I was mortified by the cowardly attempt of a terrorist to murder his Holiness the Pope..."

He was suddenly interrupted by Samir, looking grey and haunted at the back of the hall.

"My boy was not a bloody terrorist! Why do you keep throwing these inflammatory words around? He was a good boy. He loved his mother..." and instantly Samir was overpowered and smothered by Security Guards. Baz was on his wrist mobile giving instructions. Terry blanched beneath his make-up. Who the hell let that old fucker in? Cameras snapped and flashbulbs popped. This could all go pear-shaped if he wasn't careful. He needed a diversion, a few moments to regain his flow. He turned to Jocelyn and smiled. It was his cue. Jocelyn took the sheet of paper from his pocket which Terry had given him. It seemed to weigh a ton with its chicanery and dead words. He stood and on impulse turned for a moment to look at Annie. Sweet Annie who had betrayed him so horribly. Betrayed herself. Annie with her creamy skin, her butterfly kisses still lingering like tiny ghosts on his body and in his mind. It was as if every bit of her had been selected from the finest materials, a lovely delicacy beneath the worldly banter and show. She looked back at him, eyes a little moist with tears. The light caught a teardrop as it formed and silvered in the corner of her eye and in it Jocelyn saw something.

What was it? A lonely thing sitting by itself seeing nothing in particular. A shadow of a shadow. As he looked its name came to him. Regret. She smiled at him and it gave him strength. He was clearly a lousy monk, but he could be a decent man. A decent human being. That was more than enough. Who the hell was he to judge? He, who had done his best to hide from the world for so long, to hide from himself, his desires and confusions, his humanity? Others judged. Terry Bunk and his band of pirates spent their whole lives judging everyone and everything for their own dirty little purposes. They could keep it. He slowly tore up the piece of paper and stepped forward to speak.

"There was no terrorist about to kill the Pope or blow up the Vatican..." but before he could continue several things happened very quickly. Baz was about to rugby tackle Jocelyn to the ground, but before he could the Archbishop, still looking at the shaft of sunlight, suddenly sprang to his feet and pointed at the light.

"I know what it is. Look, can't you see?" He turned to Hersham Malone for confirmation. "You must see. It explains everything. Look – what's your name?" He searched his broken mind for a name to fit the face. "Macaroni. Macaroon. No, Malone, that's it, Sausage Malone. Can't you see it, Sausage? Tell them."

A ripple of laughter undulated around the room. Flashbulbs popped. Notebooks were scribbled in. Headlines were born. It was too much for Sausage Malone. His face purpled and he was on his feet. He took a step forward and punched the Archbishop full in the face, and who fell like a sack of stones to the floor. A collective intake of breath, then unabashed glee from the world's press as they started to go into shorthand overdrive. Microphones buzzed with scandal. Terry was, for once, at a loss for words, and gaping like a bloater fish. He was just about to make a quick exit, so that someone else could be found to blame for this debacle, when the Archbishop, temporarily restored to his wits by the fierce blow to the head from Sausage Malone, leaned into Terry's face and whispered "Dragon.

You murdering bastard." Then the Archbishop's face smoothed into creaseless anonymity as he slipped into a tiny corner of his mind, never to venture out again. But it was enough. If the Archbishop knew, how many others had been told? Terry had some serious spleen to vent. Baz chose precisely this wrong moment to lean into him. "Don't worry Sir, all under control," he said. Terry looked at him aghast.

"Under control. Under fucking control? With the fucking Foreign Secretary just decking the Archbishop of fucking Canterbury who's already a loony tunes. Under control, with a nerdy shit for brains monk who can't tell God from a fanny? With some daft council house Indian bloke calling me a liar to the whole world? I don't fucking think it's all under control. And you, my illiterate pug-faced twat, are sacked. As from now. Fuck off!" Said Terry, forgetting that his lapel microphone was still switched on, and that approximately two and a half billion people had just heard his tirade.

As the Archbishop was carried out on a stretcher; as Sausage was led away in handcuffs; as Terry scuttled from the room in panic; as the wires and airwaves of a million communication systems buzzed with this furnace of scandalous delights, Jocelyn went to Annie. She slipped her hand into his and they left quietly by a side door. No-one noticed, which suited them perfectly.

Chapter Thirty Two

On the other side of London Dizhwar's mother approached a Mosque, where Samir could be heard from the street, denouncing the infidels who had now shown their true colours. Liars, deceivers, war mongers, unbelievers, the trash of the universe whom God demanded be put to the fire. The vitriol flowed from him like napalm. She waited outside, listening calmly, and fingering her son's mobile phone in the folds of her jilbab, her wedding ring touching the tiny keypad. She had listened to the messages at least a dozen times – Samir ranting at Dizhwar, telling him he must blow up the Vatican or his family would perish in hell. No doubt the police would be extremely interested. First, she had a few things to do herself.

The ranting went on for another hour, but she was a patient woman. Grief and life had taught her patience and she was an expert. Finally people started leaving the Mosque, mostly young men pumped up for a fight and full of righteous indignation. She entered and went to the back. In a small private room Samir was wiping the sweat from his forehead, looking extremely satisfied with what had been an exemplary firebrand performance. He smiled at the ironic thought that a Christian fundamentalist hell and brimstone preacher would have been equally pleased with the strut and bluster of his eloquence. Shad handed him a clean handkerchief. He looked in a mirror on the wall and saw a small woman standing in the doorway behind him, and turned, curious.

"I have finished. You can go home now," he said.

"Which my son will never do again," she said, her eyes steady on him.

He sensed difficulty, but smiled. "Shad, show this woman out. I am tired." Shad moved towards her, but stopped, sensing there was more to this woman than met the eye. A sudden anger boiled in Samir. Why was there always something, just when he was really on a roll, always some obstacle, a piece of human stupidity that claimed his attention? "If you want something doing," he said, and touched her arm to lead her out. As he leaned down towards her, with the speed of a snake she gave a small jump and head butted him as hard as she could. It was an excellent blow, cracking his nose just where it met his eyebrows. He looked startled for a moment, then fell in an unconscious heap. She looked down at him.

"Next time don't call me woman. My name is Patina Abdulla, wife of Yosef, mother of Dizhwar who is now in heaven, dead because of this trash dressed up as a priest." She turned to Shad. "I know the whole dirty game. I have recordings. The police will be here soon. If I were you I'd get my skinny trembling arse out of here and hide yourself in a kebab shop and hope that God doesn't strike you down with thunder for being a part of this murdering injustice."

Shad's mouth opened and closed a few times, then he scooted out and away. Mrs Abdulla sat down heavily on the floor, a tear wetting her cheek. It was done. All that was left was that she had to see her son, her boy, her Dizhwar, to say goodbye and give him a mother's kiss to Godspeed his journey to wherever. She couldn't help but smile, thinking that those interminable hours watching Arsenal with her husband on the TV had proved helpful. A good solid header was sound preparation for decking an evil priest.

Chapter Thirty Three

What became of them all?

Jocelyn and Annie walked out of the spotlight and into each other's arms. For him, the embrace of the church had never seemed so sweet as Annie's caresses. He substituted tortuous thoughts about God with higher delights, such as Annie's breasts, her smile and kisses. The children they planned and which duly arrived, the little boy named Dizzy, the house they loved and laughed in, the science books he devoured and which proved useful in his training to become a science teacher. The Archbishop spent his remaining years smiling beatifically in a Nursing Home and consuming boxes of meringues, sent by Jocelyn once a month. He appeared to be happier than he had even been as Head of the Church, and occasionally wrote the word 'dragon' on a misty window with a trembling finger. Terry made a killing with his memoirs, which would have been more truthfully shelved under Fiction, and reinvented himself as a motivational speaker for the super rich, showing that avarice and hypocrisy will always find a profitable place in the world. Arty got a job as an Arts Council advisor, proving Einstein's maxim that one of two infinites is human stupidity. Samir spent eleven years in prison and retrained as a cake decorator. Shad became a plumber's mate. God continued to drink and smoke in the small Rome bar until he suffered a terminal stroke and was buried in a municipal graveyard – unmarked because no one knew his name. Dizhwar's parents got to see their boy one last time – by then he was no longer news so they could kiss him farewell in quiet dignity. Others rose and ebbed in the ineluctable tide of life.

The stranger, bigger picture eventually claimed all. It seems there is a wheel that turns and returns and, as in Jocelyn's new science books, everything becomes something else if you just wait long enough. Many years later Jocelyn and Annie returned as a pair of love birds, glorious in their reds and greens and blues, cosying up on a branch and singing a song only they understood, but which delighted all who heard. Terry came back as a tree grub, thinking it would consume the whole tree, but was itself eaten by a peckish sparrow and dissolved into sparrow cells forever, so some good came of him. Arty was a chubby weasel, which would seem to be a contradiction in terms – weasels should be sleek and cunning; perhaps this genetic deficiency explains why he was shot so easily by a farmer. Samir returned as a snake and in his third year made a fine meal for a mongoose. The others became – others.

If you enjoyed *Behind Closed Doors*, you might like *Bottom of the List* by Steve Attridge, also published by Endeavour Press.

Extract from Bottom of the List:

Gravity was the real enemy.

It all began when Adam Bittermouth, in his sixteenth year, lost his virginity to Rosemary Puddock in a potting shed in Ealing. His left foot had been trapped dangerously in the blades of a lawnmower and the deckchair, on which he was sitting as she bounced on top of him, collapsed. He thought he might lose a foot as well as his innocence.

He was fraught, anxiety wriggled in his veins, the smell of bodies, grass cuttings, danger and creosote creating a lethal brew that made him feel sick, and searing into some deep cellular level so that forever after grass made him tense and the woody petroleum of creosote gave him feverish sexual dreams that lasted for nights and days.

Then it happened for the first awful time. As her breasts smothered his face, he started to gag and struggle for air. He could feel the roof of the shed bearing down on him; the sheer immensity of gravity beyond the rotund dimensions of Rosemary as it pressed down and threatened to squash him like a bug.

He shouted "Oh Christ, save me!" and ran from the shed, leaving bewildered Rosemary to retrieve her knickers from a bucket of slug pellets. Outside, naked from the waist down and his gelled hair sticking out madly like satellite spikes picking up terrible messages from the ether, he fell to the ground. The sky itself was closing in. Kamikaze leaves crashed to earth, birds struggled against the weight of the universe above them, trees grew rigid and bony in their vertical toil. Everything was bearing down, pushing. It was too terrible for thought.